T0156891

The Grease Monkey

Ethel McMilin

iUniverse, Inc.
New York Bloomington

The Grease Monkey

iUniverse books may be ordered through booksellers or by contacting:

iUniverse
1663 Liberty Drive
Bloomington, IN 47403
www.iuniverse.com
1-800-Authors (1-800-288-4677)

ISBN: 978-1-4502-5582-0 (sc)
ISBN: 978-1-4502-5583-7 (ebk)

Printed in the United States of America

iUniverse rev. date: 8/26/2010

Dedication to
Myrtle and Marjorie Deaton,
our special cousins

Chapter One

Jonathon's Garage

At twelve years of age, Jonathon often baby sat with the neighbor's daughter who was five yeas old. She was a pest and sometimes would get under his skin but as long as he played games with her Lisa behaved. But it seemed that she demanded all of his attention while he was taking care of her. The tangled hair and often dirty face from playing in the dirt did nothing to make the little one attractive. He often felt sorry for her. What would she look like when she was older? One sure wouldn't call the scrawny girl pretty or attractive.

Often Jonathon worked in his father's garage. He loved it. A mechanic was what he wanted to be when he grew up. Finishing high school was the first step. He was pleased that they had a mechanic's class in high school but at the same time, he already knew everything they were teaching. But that was okay, as he needed to get an A in at least one class. He sure wasn't getting one in English.

As the years went by, he was pleased when he only had his senior year to finish high school. He worked in the evening with his father who wasn't in good health. His dad insisted that Jonathon know everything about the garage from meeting the customers to keeping the books.

"Jonathon, I'm not going to live much longer. I have signed everything over to you. You told me that you wanted to be a mechanic so you have to work hard at learning every aspect of the trade. You also have to know the business part of the job. I'll help you as long as I can but I feel a little weaker every day. I'm like you, Jonathon, I loved being a mechanic and if I spend my last hour here, it wouldn't bother me. God had given me the talent for this position long ago and I enjoyed doing the work. It now belongs to you, my son. Take good care of our garage."

The Granger Garage was only one of two garages in the small town. Each year the town grew a little and they gained a few more customers. Mr. Livingston kept pretty busy through the years and had enough automobiles to repair to make a fair living for his family.

Shortly after Jonathon graduated from high school, his father past away and he was alone in the garage. Jonathon often thought about what his dad told him. He looked like his dad, he walked like his dad, he talked like his dad, and he wanted to be a mechanic like his dad. He had been very proud of his father. Sometimes he felt that it was because his mother had passed away that his father lost his will to live.

His mother gave birth to him a little later in life than when most babies were born. His mother was in her forties and his father in his fifties.

As he worked away on his job, he knew he was going to need some help one of these days. His customers were pleased with the repair jobs he had done on their vehicles and felt that his charges were fair. They passed the word on to other potential customers. At the same time, Jonathon was making good money for someone not quite twenty. Slowly he was adding more customers. One day he'd go looking for someone to help but he wanted to be choosey. They had to know and love mechanics. He didn't want any complainers who thought the work was too hard. It appeared a lot of young people just wanted the pay check and not the work.

Jonathon thought he would start with some friends of his that needed a little work after school and in the summer. That would help him and them both. He knew that Turner Jensen wanted to go to college but had to earn his way. He was going to the local college for the first two years so he would be able to work with Jonathon in the evenings and on the weekends if needed.

Turner Jensen was hired as a part time worker. Jonathon couldn't believe how much work the young man did and that relieved him of a lot of worry about getting the vehicles done in an acceptable time.

From time to time, Mrs. Monroe would ask him to watch Lisa while she and her husband went to the doctor. She was thirteen now but they didn't want her to stay home alone. He decided to take her to the garage since he had to work that day and they agreed that that would be fine with them. Mr. Monroe had visited his garage and was impressed. It was a fine looking garage with the walls painted and the floors kept fairly clean for a garage. Yes, he liked the Granger Garage. He felt it was very safe for his daughter to spend some time there.

Mr. Monroe didn't bring his car to Jonathon's garage because if there was anything wrong with the car, Jonathon fixed it free as soon as he could right in the Monroe driveway. The family didn't have much money and Jonathon just couldn't bring himself to charge them for repairs.

Once in the garage Lisa wanted to know what this was for, why did a car need that? What was wrong with this vehicle? Didn't that look like a funny thing to put in a car? There seemed to be no end to her questions.

Jonathon shook his head.

"Lisa, what do you think I do when I come to this shop?" Jonathon asked her.

"You work on cars and repair them. I know that," she answered a little aggravated that he would ask such a dumb question.

"So if you ask me all those questions, how can I get any work done if I have to stop work to answer them?"

"Oh," she answered slowly. "I know that you vacuum and wash the cars after you repair them. Why can't I clean the cars with the vacuum cleaner? I know how to do that. Wouldn't that help you?"

"Alright, there's the shop vac and I have just finished repairing this car. Clean the inside. But be careful if you find some paper or something. It might be important to the owner. Just put it on the seat after you vacuum the vehicle," Jonathon explained.

"I can do that," Lisa exclaimed and went right to work. In about thirty minutes she wondered where the next vehicle was that needed to be cleaned. It was fun to her to vacuum a car and especially in a garage in town. That was really big stuff.

Jonathon looked at the car. It was done perfectly. He was impressed. He never thought the pesky little neighbor could do anything right other than be a pest. That was one thing she was good at for sure.

"I don't have a car that needs the inside cleaned right now but do you want to try to wash the outside of the car you just vacuumed?" he asked her. He had no idea if she knew how to do that but he would let her try if she wanted to.

"Okay, what do I use? I know my dad said if you didn't use the right thing it would scratch the car. So where are the things you use to wash the cars? I love to wash automobiles."

Jonathon stopped repairing the Buick he had been working on and got Lisa set up for washing the automobile. He could always finish the car wash if she didn't do a good job. At least this kept her busy and out of his hair. He should really have more patience with her as she only wanted to help him but sometimes her help caused more trouble than it was worth. But at least she was trying to be helpful.

Jonathon went back to work and when he finished the repair on the Buick, he went to check on how his car washer was doing. As he walked over to the vehicle and he found that she had just finished. The car was bright and shinny and definitely clean from the tires to the roof. He couldn't have done a better job himself. He was amazed. Through the years he had often wondered if the neighbor girl could ever do anything right but she sure did this time.

"Lisa, I'm proud of you. That's an excellent job. Where did you learn how to wash a car?"

"I wash my dad's car quite often. He showed me how to make it look good. I love working with cars. Dad even let me drive the car into the driveway. Three more years and I can get a permit," she answered.

"You let me know when that happens and I'll start taking the bus," he remarked and laughed.

"I'll be a good driver. At least I won't run over the neighbor's toy dog," she stated and stared at him with her hands on her hips daring him to deny it ever happened.

"If the neighbor girl hadn't left the toy dog in my driveway I wouldn't have run over it," he retorted.

Lisa laughed. "Now, boss, what's next."

"You can vacuum and clean this Buick if you wish. I suppose you know how to back it out in the yard and over by the hose?" he asked.

"I do but you're not going to let me because it's someone else's car. You're just teasing me now."

"You're right. I'll back it out for you." Jonathon was a little more impressed with his neighbor friend. He never thought she would amount to anything when she was younger but it appeared whatever she did, she did it thoroughly. The Monroes weren't well to do and barely scraped by but it appeared they taught Lisa that whatever she was doing, to do it right. The parents were good people but they were poor because Mr. Monroe could never find a good paying job.

At the end of the day before he took Lisa home, he pulled out his wallet and paid her twenty dollars. Since she had worked hard and done an excellent job he decided he should pay her something.

Lisa's eyes bugged. "Did I earn that much money," she asked excitedly. She hadn't expected him to pay her anything. He was just company for her until her parents returned from the doctor.

"You earned more but that's all you're getting," he answered and winked at the excited girl.

She held the twenty dollar bill all the way home. She hadn't brought a purse or anything so she just held it up and looked at it and put her hand down. Soon she lifted it again and looked at it. Jonathon was amused. She could have put it in her pants pocket but she wanted to look at it all the way home.

It was quite evident that Lisa never had any extra money. She must think she's rich having a twenty dollar bill in her possession. The fact was that he'd have had to pay someone else a lot more money to wash and vacuum the six cars that she did. He just might bring the pest back to work on another day.

When Lisa arrived at her home, she told her parents all the fun things she had done that day. She held up the twenty dollar bill for them to see. She was so proud that she had earned that much money.

Since their daughter liked the work so much the parent decided that she could go with Jonathon when she wasn't in school if Jonathon wanted her to.

Lisa hoped that Jonathon would ask her to go again. She had a ball that day. Maybe one day he'd let her do some little thing to repair a car. That would be so much fun, she thought.

Chapter Two

The Monroe's Problem

Turner turned out to be a very good worker and Jonathon was able to keep up with his work load. His garage was becoming very popular because of what he charged and how well he repaired the cars. He didn't want anyone to have to wait too long before he repaired their vehicle.

When Lisa was out of school on Saturday or a holiday, he always took her and let her clean and wash the cars and gave her a twenty dollar bill. She never asked for any more. She was thrilled to get that and thought it was so much fun at the garage that he shouldn't even pay her. But she didn't tell him that.

One time she caught up with him and there were no cars to clean. "Jonathon, your garage is sure messy. Couldn't I sweep it up?"

Jonathon looked at her. She sure was different than other teenagers. It appeared that Lisa loved to work and keep busy. Well, he'd just keep her busy then. "You need to use the garage vacuum cleaner because if you sweep with a broom, I'll never be able to breathe with all the dust you'll create."

"Yes, boss," she replied and went right to work vacuuming the garage and then went into the entrance way and vacuumed the whole area. She stood back and looked around. It sure looked better than it did before.

Jonathon didn't quite understand the girl. What teenage likes to work all the time? He knew she loved vehicles of all kinds and enjoyed cleaning them, but vacuuming the floor? Lisa was always a little strange growing up. She played with toy cars on dirt roads that she made instead of dainty little dolls in the house. That was why she was always so dirty looking. He used to get down on the ground and run a few cars on her roads just to please her. He guessed she just liked to be around vehicles no matter what kind they were and even if they were toys.

For many years off and on, Lisa worked in the garage. Jonathon had to admit that she was a lot of help. Vacuuming the cars and then washing them was a task that he didn't enjoy but apparently Lisa did.

Lisa was seventeen now and should be entering her senior year at her high school but that wasn't going to happen. Her parents were not in good health and they needed her to stay at home and help them. She had to cook their meals, do the wash as well as all the housework. Her mother had cancer and her father had a bad heart among other health problems.

Lisa so wanted to graduate with her class but she also knew her parents needed her at home. How could she do both? She called one of the teachers and told him her problem and why she could no longer go to school.

Mr. Richards promised to help her home school so she could graduate with her class. He'd promised to bring her all the home work she had to do and give her the appropriate tests and if she did well. "Perhaps someone else could watch your parents while you joined the class on graduation day," Mr. Richards suggested.

When she told her mother about the plan, Mrs. Monroe shed a tear. She was so pleased that her daughter would get to graduate with her classmates. Her mother knew that it wasn't fair for Lisa to stay home and take care of them but they had no other choice. There was no money to hire a nurse or someone else to do the tasks that needed to be done.

Lisa thanked the teacher over and over. She was so thrilled to be able to finish her high school courses. Mr. Richard was pleased to help the girl. He couldn't let his top student have to drop out of school because her parents needed her at home. The teacher knew that there was no money in the Monroe home to hire someone else. He was a widower and didn't have to worry about what hour he returned home at night. Mr. Richards spent his time at the Monroe home whenever Lisa needed help with her homework.

When he saw how hard Lisa worked on her lessons and did so well on the tests he knew his efforts were well worth it. He never assisted someone if they didn't really try to help themselves but Lisa was definitely working hard at completing the class work. Each time he came to the home, he bought a bag of groceries.

Mr. Richards wondered why such nice people had to go through such hard times. The house they rented seemed barely habitable. But one thing he noticed, it was always clean when he came to visit. It didn't take much to see that the parents weren't going to last too long. What would the young girl do then? He worried about her. Perhaps he could come up with some type of job when the time came.

Tyrone Richards was pleased that the neighbors were helping with groceries. When he dropped off a bag of groceries he always asked her if there were any particular food items that she needed. It seems all of the neighbors and church people brought groceries to the Monroe home as well.

He decided that Granger was a good place to live. People cared about one another and helped out when times were tough for a family. It had been that way all through the years that he lived in this town. He always returned home feeling good about helping Lisa. She was one great student and very smart.

No longer did Lisa get to go to the garage and help Jonathon. No longer did she even get to go to church. She didn't dare leave her parents. Neighbors and friends knew she couldn't be away from the home but a few minutes so they brought food to her. Without her father working there was no money coming in and everyone in the community knew that.

Mr. Jim Rover was the landlord for the Monroes and knew the situation and how ill both parents were. He let them live in the rented house without paying rent. He had already collected a lot of money from them through the years so he could afford to be a little generous now. He had heard about the doctor's report and knew it wouldn't be too long before both of the parents passed away.

He felt so badly for Lisa and wondered what the girl would do when that happened. Jim was worried about her. She was a good girl and worked hard helping her parents. Mr. Richards had told him how she was working at home on her school work so she could graduate. More power to the girl, Mr. Rover thought. It didn't hurt him to miss a couple of month's rent payments to help his friends. The house that the Monroes rented certainly wasn't the only rental he owned.

Jonathon told Lisa to give him the utility bills. He wanted to help in some way. The Monroe family and his family had always been close friends and went to the same church. When his mother and then his father passed away, the Monroes were right there to help him through it.

He felt he should do something for Lisa. He was proud of the neighborhood and the church people who provided food for the family. It was a good town that he lived in. He hated that Lisa would miss out on her senior year but was pleased that she would get to graduate from the Granger High School anyway. He could remember his graduation and it was just nice to be able to go through the graduation ceremony.

"Lisa, I'll stay with your parents on the night of graduation so you can go and graduate with your class without worrying about them. I've always have good conversations with your mom and dad when I'm there and have enjoyed visiting with them. So you plan on going to the graduation ceremony and I promise to keep your parents company." He'd like to have seen her graduate but someone that knew the family needed to be with the two sick parents.

He noticed that she was no longer the skinny little homely girl that pestered the life out of him every chance she got. While working in the garage, she became more grownup and began to fuss with her hair. There were no fancy dresses or clothes for her to wear as there was no money to buy them.

Sometimes Jonathon would give her a hand with her homework when she hit a hard subject. Sometimes he would just visit with her parents even though she was there. He was always greeted with a smile from both the parents when he came to visit.

As the school year came to a close, Lisa was excited about seeing her classmates and graduating with them. Mr. Richards saw to it she had everything she needed to graduate—gown and hat and anything else required.

When Jonathon came to sit with her parents so she could graduate with the class, he looked at her. One of the church people had purchased her a graduation dress. Lisa looked beautiful in it. When did this scrawny little outfit grow into such a beautiful young lady? And she was a lady. And she was definitely beautiful.

This past year taking care of her parents must have changed her. The bad part was that there would be no college for her, not even evening college. Going to town and getting a job would certainly be out of the question since she couldn't leave her parents. All she was going to do was stay home and help her invalid parents. He felt a little sorry for his neighbor friend.

Lisa was thrilled with her graduation time. Mr. Richards picked her up and he would bring her back home. He was proud of his student. It was a shame that there would be no college. It would be very easy for her to get a scholarship with the excellent grades she had. But she was going to have her high school diploma and he knew that was going to mean a lot to her.

Everyone one of her classmates had to greet Lisa and tell her how much they missed her during the school time. Even the boys came over and gave her a hug. She felt very much wanted. Walking up to the platform and getting her diploma was so special for the girl. Mr. Richards didn't just hand her the diploma, he had to let the audience know how hard she worked at home earning it and how she was an A student in every class. This brought a round of applause for Lisa's efforts.

After the graduation, life settled back down for Lisa. No more home work but she thought she might try some studies on line. Lisa was disappointed when she found out how much the on-line lessons cost. Well, she could find out other information on the internet by just entering the subject. That would be one way to learn.

One day Jonathon came over to visit with her. It was a Saturday and he usually took the day off unless he had a vehicle that needed to be repaired immediately. He let Turner work on Saturdays if he wanted to. He always left his phone number for Turner to call him in case someone needed him and if they appeared to be desperate to get their automobile repaired immediately.

When he came in, he sat down and visited with the parents and told Lisa to take a break. "Go to town, Lisa. Buy yourself something. Do something fun for a change and I'll entertain your parents and take good care of them." He reached in his pocket and took out his wallet and gave her fifty dollars. "No objections. Someday you can vacuum and wash some more cars for me and earn this money. Now leave," he ordered. He had looked at Lisa's tired face and knew she needed a break.

Lisa smiled. She could use a time out. He must have thought she looked as haggard as she felt. "Thank you, boss," she remarked and laughed. She wished he was her boss again. Some of her best times in her life were spent in his garage. She would love to help him again by cleaning the vehicles.

As she caught the bus to town, she wondered what to do with the money. She knew she'd buy some groceries that they needed but she thought she would buy an inexpensive dress. She wanted to save the graduation dress for special times and for church when she would get to go again. It was good to get out and have some time just for her and to walk a few places. Just walking down the sidewalk and not worrying about hurrying home was a nice change of pace.

There was a restaurant right down the block. She would take a dollar or two and buy a piece of pie and a cup of coffee and just enjoy herself. Then she would buy a dress and the rest would be spent on groceries. Jonathon probably didn't want her to spend it on groceries but there were some things she needed to be able to cook good meals for her parents.

Lisa loved her parents. They had always been good to her even though they couldn't afford to buy her the things that she needed or wanted. Her mother and she would find some good clothes at the second hand store and Lisa thought that was great. She didn't mind wearing used clothing.

If only her parents would get well, but she knew that wasn't going to happen. She had been told that it was only a matter of time before both of them would be gone. No, she wasn't going to think about that time. Lisa decided she was going to enjoy her parents while she had them.

The Monroes had a rough life. Her grandparents were very poor and her father couldn't afford to go to college and he became a laborer. He could never seem to get a good paying job but at least they paid their bills up until the time he could work no longer. That's when the neighbors stepped in and helped the family.

Walking slowly past the department store, she noticed a sale sign in the window. The few items listed on sale included dresses and blouses. Well, this was as good as any place to look for a nice dress. She walked over to the rack that had the big discount sign marked on it. One dress was marked with a low price and it was just her size and color. Then there were some genes that were marked down along with a blouse she really like.

Adding up the prices of each item, she realized she could buy all three pieces of clothing for only twenty dollars. That was one good buy. After she paid for her purchases she would pick up some groceries for her parents. Although people brought food to the house, no one bought things like baking powder, flour, yeast, spices and the like. Now she had the money to do that, thanks to Jonathon.

All the way home on the bus, she would look in the sack and view the things that she had purchased. It was nice to have some brand new clothing and some that she really liked.

She stepped off the bus as it stopped by the grocery store and purchased what she needed along with a few extra things that she knew would taste good.

Chapter Three

Taking Care of the Parents

When she arrived home, she had to show Jonathon her purchases. He saw the happy look on her face as she showed him each piece of clothing. He was so pleased that he had given her the money. She actually had earned a lot more than that when she worked for him in the past on Saturdays. He didn't intend to let her pay him back.

"Well, looks as though you have quite a few groceries as well. How in world did you manage to carry them home or even get them on the bus?" he asked. "It would have been hard for two people to carry that much."

"Oh, I know the bus driver. When he saw me with all the packages outside of the grocery store, he stopped right there and helped me carry them on the bus. Then he drove right up to the house and helped to put them to the front porch. He's a very nice man. Mr. Jonson always has been so good to me. He really likes driving that bus and meeting people and talking to them."

"Yeah, I like old Harry Jonson. He's been the town bus driver for a good many years. That was very thoughtful of him to help you with your packages. Lisa, not every bus driver would do that. Most of them would just drive off and leave you standing there or wait until you had carried the packages on the bus by yourself. They certainly wouldn't deliver you right to your home."

"I know. He's a good man."

"There are a lot of good people in Granger," he commented.

"Jonathon, it seems that everyone has been kind to us since my parents became ill. They were kind before but I mean they have been helping us and literally feeding us. I don't know what we would have done if it weren't for such nice people."

"That just goes to show you that there are a lot of good people in this world. Well, I need to get back home. You holler if you need me, Lisa. If I'm home, I'll be glad to help you and I'll be glad to give you some breaks now and then. Don't forget that. You look more rested now even if you just came from the store."

"One day I'll earn the money and pay you back. It was so nice to have it and buy some extra things," Lisa remarked.

"Lisa, I didn't pay you half of what you earned when you were vacuuming and washing cars for me at the garage. Just consider this back pay. If anyone else did that work you did, it would have cost me twice as much. So we're even," he stated and then smiled. "I did feel a little guilty letting you work so hard for so little money but you seemed to enjoy it so much I just let you do it."

"Oh, I did enjoy working in your garage and it wasn't a little money to me. It was a lot. You'd be surprised how much it helped us. I could buy a lot of things my parents needed with that twenty dollars. Thanks for being here for mom and dad. It was really nice having some time just to walk around and do some window shopping. I even had a cup of coffee and a piece of pie in a restaurant."

"I'm pleased you did that. I stop every now and then and have pie and coffee." Jonathon left feeling thankful that he had helped Lisa. He dreaded the time when her parents would be gone and he knew it wouldn't be long. He wondered how she would take it. Although she was a strong girl otherwise, how would she take their deaths? The doctor told him that he had told Lisa that the parents didn't have much more time. He hoped she wouldn't fall to pieces when the time came. All Jonathon had to do was look at the parents and he could tell that they could go anytime.

His cell phone rang and he answered it. Someone was desperate for a pickup repair so he headed for the garage. He never did mind working on the vehicles. Someone had told him that when he grew up he should try to get a job that he really liked as he would have to work five days a week. Well, he had one that he liked and on top of that, he was the boss. It couldn't get any better than that.

Once he finished repairing the pickup he headed back home. It was just a minor thing wrong with it and didn't take more than fifteen minutes to fix it. His customer sure was pleased that he repaired it right then and didn't make him wait until Monday. He had told him how badly he needed the vehicle.

Jonathon informed Lisa that he would watch her parents and let her go to church for a change. He hadn't even thought of it before. Not until yesterday did it dawn on him that she really needed a break.

Lisa was so pleased that she was going to church. She didn't want to take advantage of Jonathon but he insisted. Whenever she thought of Jonathon she always thought that he was the big brother that she didn't have. That was the way a big brother would have treated her. He would have called her a pest just as Jonathon had done through the years. He would have played in the dirt as he did with her. Yes, he was a big brother that she had known all her life.

Once she arrived at the church, many people came and welcomed her. All the people knew her situation and most of them hugged her. She enjoyed the service so much. Before the illness, she and her parents never missed a Sunday. It did feel good to be in church.

The week went by. On Thursday, when she woke up in the morning she fixed her parents' breakfast and carried the meal into their bedroom. She was shocked when she looked at her mother. Eleanor Monroe was having a very hard time getting her breath. She picked up the phone and dialed 911 and waited for the answer.

"My mother can't get her breath. Hurry! Bring the ambulance." Lisa gave her address and then went back to her mother. She patted her on the back but it didn't seem to help much.

What should she do? She had no idea. Her father was sound asleep. He slept most of the time now. She always had to wake him up to feed him. She didn't know what to do except to wait for the ambulance to come to the house. Lisa was so relieved when she heard the siren and she ran to the door.

The ambulance worker came into the house and worked with her mother. He gave her some oxygen. It seemed to help but it was only a few more minutes when she stopped breathing all together.

The doctor had ridden in the ambulance to the house since it was Eleanor Monroe. He had a special interest in the family. He tried some other things to get her to breathe but nothing worked. The lady was gone.

Lisa heard Jonathon come through the door. He had heard the siren and feared that one of her parents was gone or about to be.

"What's going on? Is your mother worse?"

Lisa only nodded.

"I'm afraid Mrs. Monroe didn't make it. She was too sick and we couldn't get her to breathe. I'm so sorry Miss Monroe. Would you like me to take her body to the morgue?" the doctor asked.

Lisa nodded in agreement again. She couldn't say anything.

She stood motionless as she watched the workers carry her mother out of the house and put her in the ambulance. She watched as the ambulance drove away with her lovely mother. The tears began to run down her cheeks.

"Lisa, I'm so sorry. Come into the kitchen and let me make you some tea. You need to sit down. Are you going to be alright?" he asked.

"I'm okay. It all happened so fast. I thought they'd take her to the hospital and she would last another day or so but she went so quickly. At least she's no longer hurting and she's in heaven now with Jesus. That's the most important part," Lisa remarked through her tears.

"You're right about that. Now is that your father talking. He must want his breakfast. Why don't I feed him?"

Lisa only nodded and let Jonathon feed her ailing father. She knew it wouldn't be long before he too would die.

Jonathon tried to get the man to talk but he never said anything anymore. He just swallowed what Jonathon fed him. Two weeks ago they had a good time talking and then all at once he couldn't seem to hold a conversation with him. The doctor said he had a stroke, dementia, along with other heart problems. It came on him fast. He had had it for some time but it appeared to get worse all at once. What a shame. Lisa can't even enjoy a conversation with her father.

"Jonathon, did you know that the funeral arrangements for both my father and mother have already been made? The church and the community took care of it. I just have to tell them when. I think I'll have the funeral on Saturday. That way they'll put it in the paper and those that are able to will come to mom's funeral. Do you think that's okay?" she asked.

"That's a good idea. Now what can I do for you?"

"There's not a lot to do. I thank you for coming over and being with me. It's strange as I knew it would happen but when it did, it shocked me. But God will take care of me. He always has."

Chapter Four

A Sad Time

Lisa stood by her mother's grave letting the tears fall. Even though she knew her mother was now released from the suffering due to her cancer-inflicted body, she couldn't help but shed tears. After watching her the last month, she should be pleased that there would be no more suffering and Lisa was pleased. But that didn't mean she wasn't going to miss her mother.

Everyone else had left except for Jonathon and he was patiently waiting for her. He was a good neighbor and he had driven her to the funeral. After giving her a hug and telling her how sorry he was for her to lose her mother, he told her to take her time and stay at the grave as long as she needed to.

He walked over to his car and waited. He wondered what she was going to do. It would only be about a month and she would be burying her father right next to her mother. His heart had given out and the doctor had given her no hope of him recovering. She would be without parents very shortly. He felt so badly for Lisa. She also would be without a home.

While he waited, Jonathon thought about their youth. He had been her neighbor all of her life. Her parents had even invited him into their house to see the new little baby girl named Lisa. He remember being so happy to have this baby live next door to him. As she grew older, Jonathon often played with her.

Being seven years older than she was, Lisa had made him into her big brother and hero. He had often baby sat her at times. Even though he was older than she was he would played her silly games with her when she was younger and she did have some strange games that she made up by herself. As far that that goes, he made up a few for her as well. He smiled when he thought about what a pest she was during those years when she was growing up.

Once her father died, Lisa would have no one and she'd have no money and no income either. A group of friends had paid for her mother's graveside funeral and they raised the money to pay for her father's when the time came.

Finally, the girl walked back to Jonathon's vehicle. He opened the door for her and she stepped inside. He wasn't sure what to say to her. "Are you all right, Lisa? Is there anything I can do for you to help you?"

"You've been so kind all ready, Jonathon. Helping me to take care of my mother and my father has taken a lot of your time but I really appreciate it. My father probably will only last a week or two. What will I do then? I have to leave the house because I can't pay the rent. There's a small life insurance policy on my dad but that's all. He had to take every last penny he had saved for medicine and rent. The doctor didn't even give him a bill for mom or himself because he knew we just didn't have it. My father hasn't worked for several months as you know. We lived off his savings for a while but the money was gone three months ago."

"Lisa, I have a suggestion. My home is a duplex and the renters just moved out. You could live there…"

"I can't afford an apartment, Jonathon. I have absolutely no money even to buy food to eat. I just don't know what to do."

"Let me finish, Lisa. If you lived in that apartment the only rent I'd charge is for you to cook my evening meal. I get so tired of ordering pizza and the like. I'm a lousy cook. I can barely boil water as they say. I'd like one good meal a day. What do you say?"

"But I'd have to find a job somewhere. I have to have money for little items. Have you any idea where I could find a job?"

“I know exactly where you can find a job. It may not be one you'd want to keep but it would bring in some money until you found a job that you really wanted to do. I know that you're a good typist and sometime you might find a secretarial position but in the mean time, you could do this other job.”

“And what is this job?” she asked curious and wondered how Jonathon had discovered a job for her when she wasn't even available for one as yet. And then what type of a job was it that he wasn't sure she would like?

Jonathon hesitated a minute. Now how was he going to tell her what the job was? He wasn't sure how she would think about this type of job but then she was desperate and would probably accept most anything. At least he hoped that she would take this job and then look around for a different one later.

“Now what's wrong with this job that you're hesitating telling me what it is?” she asked with a smile. Right now she would dig ditches for a paycheck.

“You know that I'm a mechanic and you've been to my shop several times and helped me before your parents became ill. My helper, Turner, will be quitting shortly as he needs to go to a different college to finish his degree. This college in town doesn't offer the final courses that he needs. He'll move away in a few days. It was his job to wash the cars and vacuum them after we repaired them. He could change the oil and some filters and a few other things besides keeping the garage fairly clean. Now if you don't want to try this, I'll help you find another job.”

“Oh, I think I'd like that. I remember the fun times that I had washing your cars and vacuuming them. I'll accept the job but you have to pay me a little more money than twenty dollars a day as you used to pay.” Lisa laughed.

It was good to hear her laugh. “You'll get a regular pay check every week, pest,” he remarked.

”But you do know that I have to take care of my father until…”

“Sure, I realize that and there's no hurry. I'll keep the job open. Let's make your dad's last days as comfortable as possible.” Jonathon had noticed the eager look on his friend's face when he mentioned the garage. Evidently she'd like to work there. She might change her mind after a while but this would be something that would keep her mind off her the tragedy of losing her mother. It wouldn't be long before father would be gone as well.

"As you know my dad doesn't even talk any more and he doesn't even know me. I have to wake him up to eat and I have to spoon feed him. He eats very little, not enough to keep him alive for long. And that reminds me, we better go home as I promised Mrs. Mackey that I'd come right back after the funeral. She's sitting with dad while I'm gone. She's been so good to relieve me now and then. She loved my mother and it hurt her too when mother died."

"She's a nice woman," he agreed.

Jonathon drove home and then walked Lisa over to her house. It was quiet when they entered. Where was Mrs. Morris? She glanced out the window and noticed her car wasn't parked in her driveway. As she hurried into her dad's room, she couldn't imagine her neighbor lady leaving him all alone. But once inside the room she noticed that her dad was gone.

Where was he? Then she saw a pool of blood on the floor. Lisa sat on the bed and looked around. What had happened while she was at her mother's funeral? Something terrible had happened to her father. Most likely he was at the hospital. She looked around for a note.

Jonathon put his arm around her. "Lisa, look at this note. The ambulance came and took your dad to the hospital. Evidently he was having a lot of trouble and losing blood. Now let me drive you over the hospital," he suggested.

Lisa walked numbly to Jonathon's car and slid into the seat. She said nothing. This was a nightmare. She needed time to mourn her mother and now it looked as though she would have to bury her father sooner than she thought. There was nothing to say to her neighbor friend so she just sat and let a few tears drop as he drove her toward the hospital.

"Lisa, don't worry. I'll take care of you. I'll see you through this. Remember when we were kids, I always took care of you and wouldn't let anyone pick on you. I was your big brother and I'll always be your helper."

She nodded her head. He had taken care of her while she was growing up but he wasn't obliged to keep on raising her. She was of age now and should be taking care of herself.

Then she thought about working in his garage. That sounded like so much fun. She loved it when she used to help him in the garage. And if his helper quit, he needed her. That was a good thought. Just to have someone need her made her feel better about her situation.

The two walked into the hospital and stopped at the first desk. "Could you tell me what room my father is in? His name is Jerry Monroe." Lisa watched the nurse's face. She didn't like the expression the nurse had as she looked at her. Something was definitely wrong.

"Miss Monroe, please sit right over there while I find out the information you want."

Lisa noticed that the nurse waited until she was across the room before she made the phone call. It appeared the woman didn't want to deal with her and was sending for the doctor. Jonathon and Lisa waited for five minutes.

"Lisa, stay right here. I'm going to talk with the receptionist," Jonathon informed her.

Lisa stayed put while Jonathon walked over to the desk. "Can you tell me what is going on? We just wanted his room number. Now has he passed away and is that the reason for this delay? His daughter knew that he didn't have long to live. Where is Mr. Monroe?"

"I can't tell you, Jonathon. The doctor will be here shortly and he'll talk with his daughter. There are hospital rules that I have to follow. I'm sorry but that's all I can tell you. Please take care of that young girl. I understand that she just buried her mother this morning. No one should have to go through what she's going through."

"That's right," Jonathon replied. Because the nurse wouldn't tell them where her father was, Jonathon knew that he'd died. He also knew that the hospital had to inform the relatives before they told anyone else. Evidently the nurse was supposed to give the news to Lisa. He had no problem with the nurse following the rules. He wondered if he should warn Lisa or wait until the doctor came and told her.

He looked up and saw Dr. Jensen walking down the hallway. The doctor didn't look happy. He knew the man hated it when one of his patients died and he had to tell the relatives. He had been wondering how the doctor was going to tell Lisa about her father.

Chapter Five

The New Apartment

Dr. Jensen was the family doctor and had been for years. He had delivered Lisa and could well remember the delivery. As he walked over to the young woman, he was wondering how she was going to take the latest news. He knew the family was poor and he wondered what the girl was going to do with both parents gone. It was only neighbors and friends that kept the family going once the father could no longer work.

"Hello, Lisa, how are you doing, my dear?"

"Is my father gone?" she asked bluntly.

"Yes, you knew that he couldn't last much longer. He had a terrible spell and Mrs. Mackey called the ambulance. He didn't make it to the hospital. His suffering is over, Lisa, and he's in heaven with God and your mother. If you try to remember this it will help you a lot."

"Mom said that was where she was going and there would be no more pain. It's hard to believe that God would take both of my parents and leave me here alone," Lisa remarked with tears streaming down her face.

"God doesn't just take people, Lisa. We live in a world of diseases because of sin. God mercifully let your parents die so they didn't have to suffer any longer. I'm sure He has a plan for your life."

Lisa said nothing. She could think of nothing to say.

"Lisa has a job and an apartment. My home is a duplex and she is going to rent the small apartment attached to my house. It's not very big but that's all right with her as she just needs a place to live. My renters moved out. So she's going to be all right once she gets a hold of things. Losing two parents at once hasn't been easy for her. I'm one of her neighbors and I've known her since she was a baby."

Jonathon looked at the doctor and he seemed relieved that Lisa had already found a place to live along with a job. But Jonathon wasn't about to tell him what the job was. Many people would object to a girl working in a garage. But Lisa sure didn't object. She thought it was a great idea.

Dr. Jensen was going to make a job for her if she didn't find one. He was relieved that things were going to work out for her but first she had to make peace with what had happened first. Even though she knew for a few years that she'd lose both parents, when the time came it was still hard to face. He would pray for the girl.

"Now do you want to see your dad?"

"Yes."

Lisa and Jonathon followed Dr. Jensen down the hallway to room 130. When she entered the room and looked at her dad, she thought he was just sleeping. That was the way he'd looked for the last two months. She felt his arm. She patted it. "Dad, I'm glad you're not in pain anymore," she whispered.

Lisa bent and kissed her dad on the cheek. Then she stood up and faced Jonathon. "I'm ready to go," she told him and started for the door.

"Don't we have to make funeral arrangements?" Jonathon asked.

"He's just going to have a graveside service as his wife did. I'll send his body to the mortuary and if you like, Lisa, we can have the funeral tomorrow," the doctor told her. Her mother's funeral one day and her father's the next—how was she gong to deal with it all. But perhaps it was better this way and she'd have all that behind her instead of waiting for another month to bury her father.

"I'd like that." She didn't know what else to say. She turned and hugged the doctor and whispered a thank you. Then she and Jonathon started to leave.

"Lisa, would you like something to help you sleep?" the doctor asked. The girl needed something for her nerves.

"No, thank you," she managed to say. She needed to think not to sleep. She had things to sort out in her mind. Sleep would only postpone the problems she knew that she had to face.

Dr. Jensen wished the girl would go home and sleep for a while. It would do her good but he couldn't force her to take a tranquilizer. All he could do at this point was pray for her. It was nice that her neighbor and long time friend was going to watch over her. The Livingstons and the Monroes had been friends for a good many years. Jonathon had lost his parents a few years back so he could sure sympathize with his grieving friend.

When they reached Jonathon's automobile, he opened the door for her. "Lisa, it's way past noon and you haven't eaten any lunch and neither have I. Let me take you to lunch. I know you don't think you can eat, but my friend, you have to. You don't want to become ill. We have tomorrow to go through yet."

Lisa nodded in agreement. She would try to eat but wasn't sure that she'd be able to swallow anything.

Jonathon decided to take her to the new restaurant that had just opened a few days ago. Something different would be good for her. When he drove into the parking lot her eyes lit up a bit. She had heard about the restaurant but figured it would be a long time before she'd be able to eat there. It was an expensive one that only people with money were going to patronize.

With the look on his friend's face, Jonathon was more encouraged. It never did take too much to cheer Lisa up even as a child. To him she was still a child even if she was eighteen well on her way to nineteen.

When they entered the restaurant, Jonathon asked for a table in the back. He wanted to keep her away from the crowd. She didn't need a bunch of sympathizers coming to the table trying to make conversation with her. He knew Lisa. She wouldn't like that at all.

The waitress seated them and left the menus and a glass of water for each of them. They both ordered coffee and perused the menu.

"I'm hungry, Jonathon," she exclaimed. Lisa was a little surprised at herself because she was hungry. When she first saw her dad, she didn't know if she could ever eat again and now she was ready to eat.

"I'm glad to hear you say that. What's on this menu sounds good?"

"Why don't you order for both of us? We usually like the same thing. I just don't know what I want except food."

To hear his friend be a little more cheerful felt good to him. She was actually doing better than he thought she would. He wondered if she might have considered her father had died to her when he no longer knew her or anyone and could no longer speak. That was when she really lost him. It appeared that the loss of her father wasn't as devastating as the loss of her mother had been.

The waitress returned and left the coffee pot after pouring the two cups of coffee. After they decided on the lunch, Jonathon asked her, "Lisa, I know you finished high school and graduated but you never did tell me how you did with the home schooling and Mr. Richards giving you the tests. Was it hard studying at home without a teacher? Did you get good grades?"

"I did really well with Mr. Richards helping me. If it hadn't been for him, I wouldn't have been able to graduate with my class and get my diploma. He'd bring all the subjects that I had to take to the house once a week. He gave me the tests and graded them. I have a diploma but only because he was so good to me. He was a teacher that really cared about his students. He sure spent a lot of his time bringing courses to me and grading tests and even helping me when I didn't understand a subject. I sure appreciated him. I don't know why it was so important to me to graduate from high school but it was."

"Yeah, Mr. Richards was my history teacher as well. He was a good teacher. Not just because he gave me good grades, but he's a nice man. How did you find time to do the studying?"

"Oh, my parents slept a lot and when they went to sleep early in the evening I had plenty of time to study. I really enjoyed doing the homework the teacher assigned to me. It kept my mind off my parents' bad health. I actually had a lot of time to work on the homework once the housework, cooking and taking care of my parents was done."

The waitress brought their meal and set it before them. Lisa ate almost every bite and Jonathon was pleased. She needed to eat as she still had some rough times to go through. Tomorrow wouldn't be an easy day for her.

After the meal, the two headed for home. "Lisa, I want you to look at the apartment. I think you saw it some time back when you were young and curious. Seems you pestered me to see what was beyond that door," he remarked.

"Yeah, I know I was curious and I was also a pest. You don't have to rub it in," she answered and smiled. How he ever put up with her curiosity, she didn't know but Jonathon was always patient with her, well almost always. He would even reprimand her at times if she was doing something she shouldn't.

"I want you to look at the small apartment again and see what you think. You might think it's too small. We can repaint the walls, put in new carpet, whatever you want in it. You just let me know what you want done with it to make it your home," Jonathon remarked.

"I'm sure it will be just fine as it is. You don't need to go to any extra expense for me. Jonathon, I should move in right away. I know that my folks were behind on the rent and I don't want to stay there knowing that."

"Let's move you right now. Turner is watching the garage. He'll do the things that he can and save the rest for me to do on Monday. He'll loan the customers a car if they need one. I'm sure glad I hired him. He has been a lot of help to me. It's nice to be able to leave and know some of the vehicles will be repaired while I'm gone."

"Okay, I'll take a look but I know I'll like it," Lisa exclaimed as they walked towards the apartment.

They did a quick look at the small living space and then headed next door to Lisa's home. Knowing that the furniture belonged to the landlord helped her as she didn't have to worry about moving that. Jonathon had brought some boxes out of his basement and they packed the dishes and her personal items.

"Lisa, why don't I take your parents' clothing to the Salvation Army store? Would that be all right?"

"Yes. You could do that while I finish here," she suggested.

"I don't want to leave you alone. Someone might come by and I'd like to protect you from too many well meaning people. You don't need that right now."

"Okay, we'll move everything else and then we'll load up the car with the clothes and other things that I won't be using."

By the end of the evening, the boxes were transferred to her new apartment and her old house was cleaned thoroughly. Lisa left a sign on the door for the landlord so he could locate her if he needed to. He had already excused about three months of rent and she didn't know if he was going to charge her anything more or not. He seemed like a nice man but if there was money involved, sometimes people changed their pleasant ways.

Lisa felt good that she and Jonathon had really cleaned the house from top to bottom. It was a small house and it didn't take long to clean and vacuum. It made her feel better since the landlord wouldn't have to clean the house before someone else moved in. She wanted it to look good since he'd been so kind to her parents.

Once she was in her new apartment, she sat down by the table a little too tired to do anything more. Jonathon sat down by her. They were both exhausted.

"Tell me that you don't want me to cook dinner for you tonight."

Jonathon laughed. "I'm going to order pizza for us. One last thing you have to do is make your bed. Do you know which box the sheets are in?"

"No."

"I'll get mine. Eat some pizza and make the bed and that young lady is all I want you to do tonight. You've had one rough day. Now I'm going to order us a pizza and we'll call that dinner. Tomorrow we'll also order dinner. You can start cooking day after tomorrow."

"That sounds good. You know, Jonathon, I think Dr. Jensen is praying for me. I don't know if it's because I'm busy or what, but I'm relieved my parents aren't hurting anymore and it's okay with me that they're gone. I can't believe my feelings. One thing that has really helped is that I know I have a home and a job thanks to my big brother and neighbor. I wondered what I'd do once they passed away. I figured I'd have to live on the street."

"That's the way to take the deaths, my friend and neighbor. You're still my neighbor you know. You didn't move far enough away to get away from me. And, Lisa, I would never have allowed you to live on the street. Your parents were so good to me when my parents died."

"Yeah, I'm still your neighbor and you're my landlord. How about that? But I really should pay you some money for the apartment. Just making your meals isn't enough. This apartment would bring you in several hundred dollars a month."

"Oh, cooking my meals will be plenty enough. I could hire a cook but I happen to know you're a good one. I'm very pleased with our bargain. Just look at all the money I'll be saving because I won't eat out every night or call for some food. You'll save me lots of money." He called for the pizza and then went looking for some sheets for her bed.

Together they made the bed. Lisa seemed to be a little more rested than when she first flopped down into the chair after all that cleaning and packing. Tomorrow after the funeral she would set her apartment in order.

After eating the pizza she thought about all the things that happened that day and what she had gone through. She went to her mother's funeral, saw her father's body at the hospital, packed up all her belongings at the house she used to live in and clean the house. Perhaps it was a good thing that she had so much to do that she didn't have time to think about being alone in the world. Besides, she wasn't alone. She had God to watch over her and she had her big brother who would take care of her. That was a good feeling.

Chapter Six

The Father's Funeral

"Lisa, the doctor said the funeral would be at ten. I'll drive you there. Since it will be held on Sunday there may not be too many people there on top of the fact that not too many people know that your dad passed away. This may make it a little easier for you. I know you're like me and too much sympathy only hurts all the more."

"Yes, it will make it easier. I know a lot of people loved my dad but it's so hard to try to answer all the people who offer sympathy. Some people like that and it helps them but it doesn't me. I just want to get it all over with. My parents have been dying for two years. Now I trust they'll rest in peace."

"Goodnight, Lisa, now get some sleep. Don't try to unpack anything tonight. You aren't up to it."

"I promise I'll go to bed right away, my big brother." Lisa smiled. She was glad she had someone who she could call on just as if he were her brother.

She slept much better than she thought she would since she was sleeping in a new bed and a new place. Sunday morning she was feeling pretty good. After finding what she wanted to wear to the funeral, she slipped it on and was all ready for Jonathon to come by to pick her up. He had been so kind all through her parents' illnesses and now through the funerals. What would she have done without him?

There was a knock on the door. She grabbed her purse and sweater and answered the door. "Good morning," she greeted Jonathon.

"It does look as though it's going to be a very good morning. I take it you're ready to go. I figured that you'd want to go a little early. Dr. Jensen found a minister to do the funeral ceremony. There weren't too many available since it is Sunday morning but there was an associate pastor at our church and he agreed to come."

"I didn't even think about that. It's a good thing that I didn't have to plan the funeral. I wouldn't even know where to begin. Dr. Jensen raised money for mother's and dad's funerals. He's known me all my life and I don't know how much longer than that that he knew my parents. He sure looked relieved when you told him I had an apartment and a job. I know he was worried about me."

"He's been my doctor too. He's getting up there and one of these days he'll have to retire and I sure hate that. He does have a son that's a doctor and I heard he's a good one. We might have to go to him once the doctor retires."

They reached the cemetery and walked over to her mother's grave. There every thing was set up for her father's funeral. Somehow, Lisa felt that she had some peace today. At her mother's funeral she felt as though she was falling apart. What was the difference? Was it Dr. Jensen's prayer? She wondered.

The associate pastor gave a very comforting talk as far as Lisa was concerned. She liked what he said. Maybe she would look him up at church and make sure she shook hands with him on Sundays. Her parents went to church until they became too ill. Her father took care of her mother for five years and then he failed and Lisa took care of both of them while studying for her high school diploma. It had been a hard year but she was pleased to help her parents.

Some of her friends tried to talk her into hiring someone to take care of her parents while she went to school and to some of the parties. She was embarrassed to let them know that there was no money—only enough to buy food for them. But even if she had money, she didn't think this was the time for parties. She knew they all felt sorry for her but they hadn't been through something like this so there was no way they could know how she felt. She hoped that none of them would have to go through a year like she just had.

There were only about 25 people that attended the funeral. Dr. Jensen was there and somehow she knew he would be. Some neighbors were as well. She saw the man that used to be her dad's lawyer. Was he still? There was no money to pay a lawyer so he probably came out of courtesy. He was walking over to her.

"Miss Monroe, I need a moment of your time. Your father has a small life insurance policy. I'm going to work on hurrying it up as I know you need the money. I'm so sorry that you lost both your parents so quickly. Now are you at the same place where you parents lived?" asked Gene Houston.

"No, I moved next door to that duplex. I'm renting a small apartment there. I have a job starting tomorrow," she replied.

"Oh, that is a relief. As soon as the insurance money comes, I shall bring it over to you," he promised.

"Thank you, Mr. Houston. I appreciate you telling me about the insurance. Dad mentioned it one time but I had forgotten about it. It will come in handy, believe me," she told him.

The man no sooner left when the landlord for her parents' apartment walked over to her. She hadn't even noticed him in the small crowd and hoped it wasn't money he wanted as there wasn't any to give him right now. She doubted if she had five dollars in her purse. Lisa had wondered how she was going to buy any groceries to eat without any money.

"Hello, Lisa. How are you, dear? I'm so sorry about your parents. Now I went into the house and it's very clean. Thank you for cleaning it so thoroughly. I do have some people that want to rent it and they can move right in. I want you to know that the contract was in your parents' name and not yours. I'm not going to try to collect the last three months. I want that to be my donation to you for all your problems. I'm pleased that you found an apartment where you can work to pay the rent. Have you found a job as well?"

"Yes, I have. Thank you for asking. And thank you for the three months free rent. I don't know how I could have paid you. Thank you for being so kind. May God bless you for being so thoughtful by not forcing me to make up the unpaid rent payments."

"Well, my dear, you take care of yourself. If you ever need anything, you let me know. My son, James, was asking about you. He may come to see you one of these days. I believe you two went to school together."

Lisa nodded her head. She didn't want to tell the man that his son was a... Well she wouldn't even finish the thought. She hoped that James didn't come any where near her. Lisa had all she could take from him when they were in school together. He certainly wasn't her favorite school mate.

How many others did she have to talk with? That wasn't a good thought but she just wanted to go back to her apartment and start working putting her things away. She had a new life starting tomorrow and was hoping it would be a little better than the last two years had been.

The associate pastor stopped by and shook her hand. He gave her a card. "If you ever want to talk just look me up at church," he suggested and smiled at her.

"Thank you," Lisa exclaimed enthusiastically. "I thank you for the talk you gave. It really helped me." She was pleased that he attended the same church she did. She liked the man. It was nice that he didn't repeat all the sympathetic stuff she had heard too many times already.

Jonathon didn't say too much. He watched what was going on. If someone became too sentimental as to upset Lisa he would pull her away but so far she needed to talk with the people who came by.

Dr. Jensen stopped long enough to give her a good hug and said goodbye. She did appreciate him taking the time to come to her dad's funeral. He was more than a doctor to her, he was her friend.

Lisa greeted everyone who came by the best she could but she sure wished this was over so she could go back to her apartment. This wasn't something she liked to do. She wasn't exactly a people person and she knew it. It was something she could try to work on in the future.

Jonathon was waiting for her and she walked over and stood by him. The grieving girl felt better when Jonathon was around. He had been through all this and he understood how she felt. She appreciated all their sympathies but they just brought more tears to her eyes.

Finally everyone began leaving the cemetery. Lisa stayed by her father and mother's grave for a short time. Now that the people were gone, she just wanted to stay there a little longer. Jonathon had said to stay as long as she wished. It seemed a little foolish to her to just stand there and look at the graves. But as foolish as it was, she said a goodbye to her mom and then to her dad. She told them that she missed them both but she was pleased that they were in heaven now without any pain.

Finally she decided that it was time to leave. Jonathon had been so good and it wasn't right to keep him waiting for her. She walked over to the automobile where he was standing.

He hugged her and opened the door for her to slip into the vehicle. They were on their way to her new home. As she thought about it, she knew that it was going to be a good thing that she had a whole new atmosphere to live in. Everything was different. That would help her with her sadness concerning her parents.

Chapter Seven

Working in the Garage

Once she was back in the apartment, she went right to work. After an hour Jonathon stuck his head in the door which she had left open and told her he was bringing their dinner. He thought he'd get a bucket of fried chicken if that was all right with her. That's what sounded good to him.

"That sounds good to me too. I've made a lot of headway putting things away. Step in and look around."

Jonathon did. "You've done a lot. It doesn't look as though you have too many more things to put away. Have you thought about painting the walls?" he asked.

"Maybe a little later on I will but not now. I'm anxious to go to work with you tomorrow and see what all you're going to let me do. It should be fun. I sure enjoyed the times I came to visit you there. You know, Jonathon, just the fact that I have a place to live and a job makes me feel warm inside. I worried so much about that when I knew my folks weren't going to live. I couldn't get away from the house to look for work. The grocery man was so kind to send a boy out to deliver the groceries and he certainly didn't charge what he was supposed to."

"Lisa, sometimes it does a person good to give a little charity. If anyone needed it you did. So just be thankful that your parents had good friends in the community that wanted to help you. Now I should be back in about fifteen or twenty minutes. You won't starve by then will you?"

"I think I can wait that long but not much longer," she answered laughing.

It was good to see Lisa laugh, Jonathon thought. She was actually doing quite well considering what she had been through. He knew she was a strong girl but to lose two parents at once was hard thing to have to go through.

After looking over all the boxes, Lisa decided to work on putting the dishes away. They were clean as she had wrapped them in clean paper. She didn't intend to rewash them. That didn't take too long and then she worked on her personal things. In the bedroom was a desk with a cupboard right above it. That was a good place for her prize possessions—things her mother and father had for keepsakes.

That took a little longer but she just finished the job just before Jonathon knocked on the door.

"Come in."

"This smells so good we have to eat it now. Whatever you're doing, stop right now." He set the bucket on the table and found two plates and two forks.

"It sure smells good to me as well." The two ate pretty much in silence. Lisa couldn't remember the last time she had some fried chicken.

"You're just about through with your unpacking. Well, I want you to get a good night's rest as I intend to work the day lights out of you tomorrow," Jonathon warned her with a grin.

"Yeah, I can see that. I hope you show me a few things about cars. Oh, we should pull my folks' car over here. It doesn't run anymore. You wouldn't have any extra bay in the garage to park it in and maybe I could work on it if you told me what to do," Lisa suggested. She sure wanted to have a car if she needed to go some place other than the garage.

"Not a bad idea. We'll do that after we eat. I'll take a look at it first. Do you have your driver's license?"

"Yes, I got them when I was sixteen. I haven't been able to drive much, though. I did go after some medicine for my folks two or three times."

"If I get it running, I'd still want you to bring it to the shop and let me look it over. With it sitting so long without running, a number of things can happen." Jonathon told her.

Lisa nodded her head. If it would only run, she could sure use a car. She thought about it some more. She loved to drive. There wasn't a car around that Jonathon couldn't fix so she knew he could fix hers. She just had to be patient and wait until he had time to fix it.

As soon as they had finished eating the chicken and cleaned up the table, they walked over to the vehicle. Jonathon raised the hood and looked around. He bet a good cleaning would do it a lot of good. He took the key from Lisa and stepped into the car and started it. It took a few tries but it did start. He looked at the gas tank—almost empty. The oil was way down. He had oil at his apartment and he would put some in the car. He didn't like driving any car where the oil was that low.

When the car started right up, Lisa smiled. She had a car of her own. Jonathon had talked about loaning her one, but she would much rather drive her own vehicle. Driving someone else's automobile would make her nervous.

"Now don't get too excited, Lisa. It still needs some work. I'm putting in some oil to get it to the gas station and then we're going to change the oil. Let me say that differently. You're going to change the oil."

"Really," she exclaimed and smiled. She always wanted to know about cars—anything about them. Changing the oil on a vehicle should be fun.

It was bright and early the next morning when Jonathon knocked on her door. There was her car, right out in her driveway.

"Since you know where the garage is, I'll follow you to work just to make sure you get there in this vehicle. I guarantee nothing about it but it should make it to the garage."

Lisa stepped into her car and drove toward town. She knew she was probably going way too slow for the man who was following her but it had been some time since she had driven a car anywhere. Finally, she arrived at the garage and parked her automobile in front of the first bay door and then stepped out waiting for Jonathon to park his vehicle. It sure was a lot newer one than hers but she didn't care. She had a car and that was what was important to her!

Jonathon walked with her into the garage office. She introduced her to Sylvia Dawson. "Sylvia, this is Lisa Monroe. She's going to be working here. Lisa is my neighbor. I used to baby sit her."

At that remark, Sylvia laughed. "Is that right? She still looks pretty young and might still need a baby sitter."

Lisa didn't know how to take that remark so she just laughed. "It's nice to meet you, Sylvia. I guess we'll be working together."

"Well, not quite. I'll be in the office and you'll be in the greasy old garage." Sylvia made the statement and looked at Lisa.

"I know. I'm so excited about learning how to repair the different vehicles. I had signed up for auto mechanics in high school and then I had to drop out of high school and take care of my parents. But I'm going to watch my big brother here work on cars and then I'll learn a few things."

"He's a good mechanic, the best one in town. You can ask about anyone that and they'd agree that he was."

There was something about Sylvia that Lisa didn't quite understand. She had a feeling that Sylvia thought Jonathon was her property. That was why she added the big brother bit. She didn't want to start off wrong with the only other girl in the garage. She hoped to make friends with her.

The day couldn't have been better. Jonathon had provided her with plastic gloves to protect her hands. She cleaned the garage, washed down several cars and cleaned them inside and then changed the oil in her car. She was thrilled.

"You need to change the air filter."

"What's the air filter?"

"That thing right there," Jonathon said and pointed to the filter. "Now see if you can figure out how to take it out."

This was right down her alley. She always liked to figure out puzzles. Lisa looked it over carefully and finally took the old filter out of the car. Jonathon was impressed.

"Now put a new one in the same way you took the old one out. After you do that take that cleaning fluid and clean up a little of that dirt under the hood on some of the cables. That dirt isn't good for a vehicle."

It took her a little while but soon she had the engine looking pretty clean. She went ahead and washed her car and vacuumed the insides.

"Okay, boss, what's next?"

"A car just came in that needs an oil change. Pull it up on the lube rack and see if you can figure out how to change the oil."

Since the car belonged to someone else, Jonathon watched her carefully. She did everything just like he would have. In no time she had the old oil out and the new oil in. He noticed that she didn't have a drop on herself or her clothes. He always managed to get some on his coveralls.

When he had given her a pair of coveralls to put on, she'd given him a strange look but she put them over her clothes. He was the boss and she would do as he said. She didn't think the coveralls were very flattering but that was okay. It didn't matter what she looked like repairing cars.

"Now, write up the bill."

"Write up the bill? Let's see. There looks like a pad of potential costs for repairing vehicles. There's a list of what the customer has to pay some by hour and some by the task." She wrote down the number of quarts of oil that she used plus the cost of the mechanic. There was a set amount for changing the oil. "What's the man's name?"

"Sam Jones."

She filled that in and looked for his address and included that. "Well, boss, is this right?"

"It's perfect. You're going to make a great grease monkey."

Lisa burst out laughing. She had heard mechanics called grease monkeys before and now she was one—well not quite but almost. She intended to learn every task connected with the cars.

"Now take the bill and the car key out to Mr. Jones. But first, I think you should lower the car from the lube rack and drive it outside the garage."

"You think so?" She did and handed the keys and the bill to Mr. Jones. He wrote out a check and Lisa took it to the office.

"I've never had the work done so fast before. He must not have a lot of cars right now," Sam remarked.

"He does but he has some extra help. That speeds up the process," Lisa informed Sam. She was pleased that Sam was happy about getting his vehicle so quickly. She wasn't about to tell him that she did the oil change.

Sam Jones left feeling very pleased. He was in a hurry anyway but he assumed he would have to wait his turn. That Jonathon was one good mechanic. He had recommended him to several people when they needed their vehicle repaired.

Lisa decided that a cup of coffee sounded good so she poured herself a cup and sat down on the bench and drank it.

In only a few seconds Jonathon came out of the garage and into the room. "Now where's my grease monkey?" he asked.

"Right here, boss, just taking a short break for a swallow of coffee. You know it is the law that we get fifteen minute breaks."

Jonathon looked at her and laughed. "Pour me one while you're at it. Then we'll work on that car that I think just drove in. Can you ask the man what he needs done with his vehicle?"

"Sure," Lisa replied.

She took her coffee with her as she walked out of the garage door and greeted the new customer. He told her that his car wasn't running right and he wanted Jonathon to look it over. He could leave it there for two days but he hoped to pick it up after that. He had a friend who would take him home.

"Leave me your name and phone number and I'll have Jonathon take a look at it. He'll give you a call and let you know how long it will take."

"Fair enough," the customer replied.

He handed her his card and drove off. So that was Joe Bentley. Somewhere she had heard that name before but couldn't remember when or where. She hadn't paid much attention to the vehicle but turned to look at it. Wow. It was a Mercedes Benz. She would sure like to drive that into the garage and put it in one of the empty bays.

When she walked back into the reception area, Jonathon was right there. "You handled that just fine, Lisa. So Mr. Bentley thinks his Mercedes isn't running right. Well, let me take a look." Jonathon listened to the motor. It appeared to him to be a minor thing that he could fix right away but he decided to let Lisa do it.

"Pull the car into bay four," he ordered.

Really, she was going to get to drive that Mercedes. Wow! She drove it right into bay four as ordered. In all of her life, she didn't believe that she'd ever drive a car like the one she had just driven into the garage.

Jonathon raised the hood while it was still running. "This timer is a little off. This is what you do." He explained it to her and she did exactly as he said. It took a little while but soon the engine was purring like a kitten. She smiled. Her first real repair on a vehicle other than her own and it was a Mercedes Benz.

"You call Mr. Bentley and tell him that it was a minor thing and it will be ready when he wants it. But first make up the bill. There is no need to clean it as he keeps it clean as a whistle. And I wouldn't dare try to wash his car. He's very particular about that and he washes it himself. Most people appreciate taking home a clean car but not everyone wants someone else washing their car."

She wrote up the bill without any problems at all. She showed it to Jonathon just to make sure. She was never quite sure how much to charge the customer when it was something minor that was wrong. Then she called up Joe Bentley and told him exactly what Jonathon said to tell him.

"You mean that I can pick up my Mercedes today? I knew that Jonathon was a good mechanic, but I didn't know he could work that fast," Joe Bentley exclaimed.

Just about the time they were to close the shop, Mr. Bentley came by for the car and not only paid the bill but left a good size tip for having it done so quickly.

Jonathon told Lisa that he wanted her to leave her car there until he had time to make sure every thing was as it should be. So the she rode home in Jonathon's vehicle that afternoon.

"Well, how did you like your first day on the job?" Jonathon asked.

"I loved every minute of it. I learned so much in just one day. And look at my hands, they are clean. I'm so glad you have those plastic gloves for me to wear. I wouldn't want my hands looking like I've seen some mechanics hands look."

"I have a present for you," Jonathon remarked and handed her a book on automobile mechanics. Now don't spend all your time reading this but study a few pages each night. If you sit up all night looking at it, you won't be any good for me tomorrow. It's really quite a good book and explains the repair in easy language."

Lisa's eyes lit up. She'd sure read it thoroughly because she wanted to know everything she could about the work she was doing. Oh, she knew it wasn't what most women wanted to do but she wasn't like most women. More than once, she'd been told that and to her it was a compliment.

It didn't take her too long to fix their evening meal. She had a cook book with a lot of fast meals and they were tasty. Jonathon was very pleased with what he had for dinner. He had given her a credit card and told her to use that to buy the things they would eat. Well, that made sense to her. Otherwise she would always be asking him for money for the groceries for him and for herself.

"Lisa, if you ever find another job somewhere, it's okay to take it." Jonathon didn't want her to think she had to keep this one. He wasn't sure if she had some other goal in life or what.

"You trying to get rid of me already, boss?" she asked.

"No, I'd like to keep you, but I want you to do exactly what you want to do. I don't want you to feel you have to stay in the garage just because we're friends. But if you want to stay, I'd be very pleased."

"I want to be a grease monkey," she exclaimed.

Jonathon laughed. "Okay, you have the job for as long as you want it." Lisa always was different than other girls. When she was younger at times that fact made her a nuisance but not anymore. As he thought about her wanting to stay and work in the garage, he was very pleased.

"Lisa, tell me how did you like Sylvia?" Jonathon asked because he had heard the barbs that the woman was slinging in Lisa's direction.

"Well…she's a little hard to take sometimes. I haven't quite figured her out yet but I would like to make friends with her."

"You better forget about that. You'll never make friends with her. She's not the type to make friends and she's definitely not your type," Jonathon informed her.

"But she is very friendly with you, so why not me?"

"Yeah, a little bit too friendly." That was all Jonathon said about the woman who sat in his garage office. He had given her a job when she needed one, but Sylvia refused to do the clean up or anything other than sit in the office and do the bookkeeping. He wasn't exactly happy with her.

He intended to watch her and make sure she didn't give Lisa too bad a time. He had known the young woman before. He knew she wasn't someone who liked people but he felt so sorry for her because she couldn't find a job so he gave her one.

How many times had he asked her to clean the reception area? But she always said she was too busy and she'd get to it later. She wasn't worth the money he paid her but he did have to admit that she was a good bookkeeping.

Jonathon had often looked over the books and found that she did them up right. That was one thing in her favor.

Chapter Eight

A Problem with Sylvia

The next day Lisa was working away in the reception area. Jonathon remarked how untidy it looked and asked her to clean it up a little. He told her that Sylvia was supposed to clean that area but about all she cleaned was her office and didn't do a very good job of that. Lisa only took about an hour and the place looked pretty spruced up.

Jonathon came out and looked around. "Well, grease monkey, it's nice to see that you are thorough in whatever you do. The place never looked better. He said it loud enough for Sylvia to hear."

She smiled at him and happened to look Sylvia's way. She was throwing daggers at her. Now what did she do to that woman? It appeared that if she even talked with Jonathon, it upset Sylvia.

Lisa went back into the garage and changed oil and rotated the tires on a car. Afterwards she went back to the reception area and poured a cup of coffee. Those tires were a little heavier than she thought but she had told Jonathon she could handle them. It was just a matter of building up a few muscles to lift the heavy items. She sat down and just as she did she saw Sylvia coming toward her.

"You know that Jonathon is taken, don't you?"

"What are you talking about?" Lisa asked.

"There's no sense in you trying to make up to Jonathon. He's taken. Stay away from him."

"Sylvia, Jonathon and I are neighbors. I've known him all my life. He's my big brother. He has a right to have all the girl friends he wants. We're friends, good friends, but that's all."

"Well, if you fall for him, you'll only get hurt. Now I suggest you be a little less friendly to him."

"I'm afraid I don't understand. If I change the way that I've acted toward him all my life he's going to wonder what's wrong with me. He'd probably ask me if I was mad at him. Do I tell him that Sylvia said…?"

"Don't you dare say anything like that to Jonathon now or ever. But mark my words, you'll be sorry if you start going out with him. You'll just get hurt."

Lisa quickly swallowed her coffee, even though it was a little hot, and hurried back to the garage. There was a vehicle in bay two that needed the air filter changed. She would take care of that. She was pleased to see Jonathon working under a vehicle. She didn't want him to hear what Sylvia had told her. It would probably make him mad at the secretary.

"Hey, grease monkey, you have that filter changed?"

"Yes, boss, it's done. I'm working on the second one now." For some reason she loved it when he called her grease monkey. She knew he meant it as a compliment and a tease as well. It made her feel as though she really was a mechanic.

"Good. Now come under this car. I want to show you something."

Lisa crawled under the car. Why didn't he put it over the lube rack so he could stand up and try to fix it?

"See that wire?"

"Yes, it should be hooked to something but what?" she asked.

"Right here," he answered and showed her the place and gave her time to look it over.

Lisa looked and thought that it made sense that the wire should be connected to the place a few inches away.

"Don't just look at it, hook it up," Jonathon ordered with a smile.

"Yes, boss," Lisa answered and smiled. She put the wire back to where it should be and made sure it was secured so it couldn't come out again.

The second day was finally over.

"Still like your job?" he asked.

"I love it. Hey, I never did ask what kind of pay I get."

"Pay, you expect some pay for having so much fun?"

Lisa laughed. He told her how much she would receive and she was shocked. She could never make that much money working any where else. Besides there would never be any job that she would enjoy as much as she enjoyed this one.

"Lisa, I'm glad you didn't ask me the first day because I'd have given you a much lower amount. But you've proven yourself and I can see that you're going to be one great mechanic. I see you learned a number of things from the book I gave you. I've had several men so pleased because we did the work so quickly. I'm afraid I didn't give you credit for the work. Some men are strange. If they thought a woman fixed their automobile, they wouldn't be pleased and would look for something wrong. I don't think they believe in women mechanics or should I say women grease monkeys?"

"Is that right? Then I wouldn't tell them. Anyway I hope I'm worth as much money as you're paying me. That's a lot of money."

"You've made out a few bills. You can see that we do bring in a good amount of money every day. The thing is that we charge less than they do at the other garage across town or garages in the surrounding towns and still we make a good profit. You, my little grease monkey, earn every penny that I'm paying you."

Lisa fixed the dinner that evening. Before she left that morning she had put a roast along with vegetables in the crock pot and set the timer. She knew it would be done and shut off when she returned home but it would still be hot. She checked the pot roast and it was just the way she wanted it to be.

They visited through the dinner. "Lisa, you have only a small kitchen. Are you sure you don't want to use my kitchen to cook. I have a lot more pots, pans, and things to cook with. My mom loved to cook and had about every thing a cook would want. You look and see if you can use any of the items she had."

"I might try that tomorrow," she suggested.

The first week went by real fast. She felt so good about her job. She was a very careful person always wanting to do things perfect. That was the way she did her mechanic work in Jonathon's garage. It was so nice when he complimented her. She didn't want him to be disappointed because he had hired her. So far he seemed very pleased with what she accomplished.

"Are you going to go to church Sunday, Lisa?" Jonathon asked.

"I wanted to. Would you go with me?" she asked.

"Sure, I don't know why not. Now I have to go to the garage for about two hours on Saturday to meet a man and discuss some things with him. He has this experiment going and wants my advice. But you stay home and rest and cook me a good dinner for tonight. Or you can take your car and go shopping if you want."

"Oh, I'll just stay home. I see our yard needs a little work. I may rake it. I love the outdoors."

"Suit yourself."

Sometime after Jonathon left, she did go work in the yard. He had a nice yard but it was sadly neglected. He didn't have time to take care of it. As she worked away, she noticed that James was coming her way. If he hadn't seen her she would have gone back in the house but he did see her. She had to be polite if only for his father's sake, certainly not for him.

"Hello, Lisa. It's so good to see you. Now that you're free from having to be a slave to your parents…"

"I never felt like a slave to my parents. I loved helping them. I'm sorry they're gone. They were very good parents, James, and it was an honor for me to help them." She made the remarks sternly. He acted as if she should celebrate because she was free from them.

"Well, what I wanted was to take you out on a date. That's what I mean by being free. Let's go tomorrow and I'll show you the town. I know you've been cooped up for a long time and going out and seeing the town would be good for you," James suggested and smiled.

"I've already seen the town and I have other plans for tomorrow. Sorry," she responded.

"What plans?"

"If you must know, I'm going to church. Now if you want to come along, you're welcome." Lisa watched his face form a frown. She knew he hated anything to do with churches, Christians or anything religious even though his father was a Christian.

"You have to be kidding. I…"

"No, I'm not kidding. I'm going to go to the church where my folks and I went for so long. I really like that church and the associate pastor spoke at my dad's funeral last week. It's a good church. You might even enjoy it. You wouldn't know if you liked it or not unless you attended one time."

Ignoring what she said, he stated, "I'm sorry that I missed the funeral services for your mom and dad."

"The ministers did a good job at the funerals," Lisa answered.

"What about right after you get home from church?" he asked.

"I'm sorry but I have plans for the whole day."

"Well, then we'll just go out on Monday. Be ready by ten o'clock and I'll pick you up," he demanded and started to walk away.

"Sorry but I have a job as I'm a working girl now. I'll be working Monday all day. I'll be too tired to go any where Monday night. Now, I'm going to put this fact to you bluntly, James. I wouldn't go out with you if I were free. You and I aren't friends. We don't agree on anything and a date just wouldn't work out. I would only date a man who was a Christian and someone with whom I had something in common."

"After my dad forgave you all that rent money, you talk to me like that? You'll go out with me or you'll pay the back rent money. You can pay it to me."

"I didn't sign the contract, my parents did. Your dad made it plain that I didn't have to worry about that. Now if he changes his mind, he'll tell me and I'll pay him and not you. Now goodbye, James, I'm busy."

She continued to work in the yard. She brought the mower out and began to mow the lawn. He walked over to her and turned the mower off.

Lisa stared at him.

"You're going out with me if I have to kidnap you. Now I asked you all through the years at school and you'd never go but now you're going with me and I don't mean maybe. There's not a reason under the sun that you can't date me one evening this coming week."

"I don't think she's going anywhere with you, James. You're on my property and I want you off right now." Jonathon walked over toward

James and looked down on him. James was a small man and Jonathon was much taller.

James started walking away. "This isn't over," he yelled and left.

"Is he an old boyfriend?" Jonathon asked.

Lisa visibly shivered. "Oh, what a terrible thought. All through school I turned him down and for some reason he thought I'd go out with him now. I don't understand the man. He figured because his dad forgave the rent money that made him eligible to be my date."

"I hope you don't feel that way about all men as I was going to ask you to go out with me to have dinner Sunday. Are you going to turn me down?" Jonathon was smiling at her. He actually knew James and knew what a creep he really was. He had great parents but he sure didn't take after them.

"No, of course not, you're my boss. I have to do as you say," Lisa answered with an ornery smile.

"Is that the only reason you'd go out with me?"

"Now, Jonathon, that's a silly question."

"I'm just teasing you. Is dinner about ready or should I say lunch."

"It's in the oven," she replied. They both walked into the house.

After dinner, Jonathon helped her clean up the kitchen. "You know you don't have to help clean up. I'm supposed to be earning my rent by fixing your meal and cleaning your kitchen. I think I should clean the rest of the house as well and the yard. You're a busy man."

"I like to help you clean up. I enjoy your company. We don't get to visit a lot at the garage. We're both a little too busy. Lisa, remember when we were kids?"

"Yes," she answered.

"Whenever I would leave, you insisted on giving me a hug." He walked over to her and gave her a hug. "That's our new ritual for the evenings."

"That's a good idea," she said nonchalantly and headed for her apartment. She had some things to do tonight as she wanted to be free Sunday. Now what should she wear to church? Perhaps she would wear her nice graduation gown. She wanted to wear something nice since she would be with Jonathon.

It was going to be nice to be able to attend her church every Sunday and even participate in some of the church activities. It had been too long since she was able to do that. She had lots of friends at the church.

Perhaps they could find some couples that would want to go to dinners with them and make it a church affair. They used to do that a few years ago.

Chapter Nine

Sunday Dinner

Sunday morning Lisa was all ready to go to church when Jonathon knocked on her door. She walked out with him to his nice automobile. She noticed him looking at her and smiling. She wondered if there was something wrong with her dress.

"Say, you sure look nice. After seeing you all week as a grease monkey, this sure changes your looks. That was your graduation dress, wasn't it? I remember the night you put that on. It's a beautiful garment on a beautiful girl."

Lisa said nothing but smiled. Jonathon liked to tease and he always teased her while they were growing up. She assumed that he'd keep it up as long as she knew him or was around him.

They entered the church and Lisa was surprised to find so many people that they knew. Many of her neighbors, friends from school, some of her parents' friends were there and gave her a hug and welcomed her. That pleased Lisa. The Sunday when Jonathon volunteered to stay with her parents was the only Sunday she had been to the church in years due to her parents' health. It was nice to see so many people that she knew coming to the church now. It had grown significantly from the time she and her parents used to attend.

At least she wouldn't necessarily be an unknown at this church. Lisa glanced at Jonathon from time to time and he sure was taking in everything the pastor said. Both of them enjoyed the service and determined that they were coming back every Sunday. There was nothing stopping her now from going each Sunday.

Jonathon had been a little careless with his church attendance but he decided he would change that. It was good to be in church. It was good to see his friends. He felt as though he should have been a little more faithful in his church attendance and in the future he would be. He knew that Lisa was enjoying the service as he looked at her face several times. The service was doing her a lot of good.

"That was a good service, Lisa. I like that preacher. He talks like his associate that spoke at your dad's funeral. I really want to learn a little more about what they believe. It appears they believe the Bible and that's good. That's what I believe although I've never read it all the way through. You know what, my little grease monkey, we should have a daily Bible reading right after lunch. The pastor sure encouraged us to do that."

"Wouldn't that be nice? I'd like to know a little more about what he preached on. He said to start in Matthew. Let's do that." Although she had gone to church through the years and considered herself a Christian, she hadn't read the Bible all that much. Now was a good time to begin doing just that.

"Are you ready for a meal you don't have to cook? I think all Sundays we should eat out."

"I'll agree with that. Where are we going?" Lisa asked her friend.

"Let's try that restaurant on State Street. I think it's a family restaurant. I ate there a few times and the food was good," Jonathon informed her. "They also have some very nice waitresses."

"You mean to tell me, Jonathon Livingston, that you judge a restaurant not by how good the food is but by how good looking the waitresses are? That's interesting," Lisa remarked.

Jonathon looked at her and just shook his head.

When they entered the restaurant they were surprised. It looked as if half the church was in the restaurant. Lisa saw one empty table and hoped that they would get that. The waitress came over and led them to the table leaving each a glass of water and the menus for them to peruse.

Several of the church people came over and said hi to them. "We always go out on Sundays. We're glad you could join us. Let's scoot your table a little closer to ours so we can visit," Jim McAfee suggested.

Jim and Jonathon moved it close to the other tables.

This was nice, thought Lisa. They had found friends already. She knew that the group thought that she and Jonathon was a couple. Well, that's all right. Let them think that if they wanted to. They came to church together and they would be coming every Sunday together. It would be hard to explain that he was like a big brother to her and that they weren't a couple. It wouldn't hurt anything if they did consider the two of them as closer friends than they were.

It was after three o'clock before they left the restaurant. Everyone wanted to visit with them. The owners didn't mind at all. They had ordered desert and ate it slowly. When it was time to leave, Lisa was rather sorry. It was such a good time. While she was tied up taking care of her parents, she had lost contact with all her friends. It was good to visit with them now.

Once they returned home, Jonathon told her that she didn't have to make any dinner that evening. He was too full and he'd make a sandwich and that was all he wanted. But she was welcome to come in and watch a movie with him.

"All right, I'll do that. I wanted to see that movie they talked about at the restaurant. It sounded like a good one. She came in and he led her to the love seat.

"We're at the movies and on a date and we have to act that way," Jonathon explained smiling at her in his mischievous smile. He looked at her and waited for her to say something.

"Oh, I didn't realize that. Well if we're at the movies then where's the bag of popcorn?"

"Just a jiffy and it will be ready." He slipped a package into the microwave and soon brought it with a couple of juice drinks.

"So we're ate the movies. It looks like we have a few minutes before our movie starts." Lisa grabbed some popcorn and drank some juice. She wasn't in the least hungry but they were at the movies so she was going along with Jonathon.

"Now, I have to put my arm around you because we're on a date."

She gave him an ornery smile. She couldn't help but think what Sylvia would say about their movie date. No way was she going to inform her. Jonathon sure liked to tease her and that was what he was doing now.

They laughed through the film and commented and Lisa all but cried in one of the sad places. Jonathon pulled out his handkerchief and wiped a tear away.

When it was over, he gave her a hug. It was late and they had to work the next day. It was definitely bedtime.

She went to her apartment. Everything she did with Jonathon was fun. Lisa was ready to go back to the garage. During the week she had studied the book that Jonathon had given her. It sure helped when it came to working with the cars. It was a huge book and it would probably take a year to finish studying it. She took it slow and made sure she understood every thing in one chapter before she went to the next to learn how to repair another item.

When they arrived at work that Monday morning, it appeared to Lisa that Sylvia was in a fowl mood. She just glared at her. When Jonathon disappeared into the garage Sylvia gave her another warning.

"I told you to stop chasing him. I heard you had lunch with him yesterday. Now, he's going to marry me so you keep your hands off of him. I've been here over two years and I have seniority. Now I don't want to hear of you going out with him again, do you understand?"

"Sylvia, we went to church and then went out to eat with a whole bunch of other church people. You'd have been welcome to come. Why don't you come to church with us next Sunday and go out to lunch with the group. They're really very nice people and I know you'd enjoy them."

"I just might do that. Now you better get to work."

"Yes, ma'am," Lisa replied and saluted her. She laughed all the way into the garage. Somehow, Sylvia had the idea that she was Lisa's boss. Lisa just went along with it. It didn't hurt to soothe Sylvia's feelings and let her have a victory or two. As long as it was good for the garage and Jonathon approved, she'd do whatever Sylvia told her to.

Jonathon came over to her when she stepped in the garage. "I heard what Sylvia said to you. It's not true. I'd never marry someone like her. Now someone like you would be different." With that said he went back to work.

Lisa shook her head. Now what was it he said? He'd never marry some one like Sylvia. Well, she knew that already regardless of what Sylvia told her. She could tell she was definitely not his type. She wasn't even a Christian and no way would he be interested in her. That was the very reason that what Sylvia told her didn't bother her one bit. She hoped when Jonathon chose a woman to marry it would be a real nice one who was a Christian and someone with whom she could be friends.

But then he said he'd marry someone like me. That was a strange thing to say. She wondered why he said something like that. It didn't matter but why did he say that? Then she thought that he was teasing her again.

Again she enjoyed the day. After she finished a job, she headed for a cup of coffee.

"Hey, grease monkey, where are you?" he asked as he stepped into the reception area.

"Why do you let him call you that, Lisa? You don't have to take that," Sylvia remarked.

"I don't mind it. That's exactly what I am, a grease monkey. He's not trying to insult me, Sylvia. As you know Jonathon just likes to tease me."

"Where's my coffee," Jonathon asked.

"Right here, boss," she stated and quickly poured him a cup.

All week long, she put up with Sylvia's sharp remarks. Jonathon heard most of them and begged her to ignore the unhappy woman. He hated to let Sylvia go, but if she couldn't get along with Lisa, she wouldn't be able to get along with too many other people. She only got along with him because she had a crush on him and he knew it but he did absolutely nothing to encourage it.

But all in all it was a good week, Lisa thought. When she cooked dinner that Friday night, again he helped her with the kitchen and then turned to leave.

"Hey, you forgot something," Lisa exclaimed.

"What?" he asked.

"Where's my hug?"

Jonathon laughed. He didn't know if she liked him hugging her or not so he thought he'd find out. He came over and hugged her. "Come watch television with me. I'm too tired to do anything else."

She agreed and they sat on the love seat again and watched different programs. They didn't have to get up early in the morning. Jonathon only worked Saturdays when someone called him and needed a rush job.

As Jonathon turned the television off, he gave her another hug. Then he kissed her. "I thought we should add that to our nightly ritual," he remarked as she turned and headed for her apartment. She turned around and looked at him and he was still watching her.

"Goodnight Jonathon," she stated shaking her head.

"Goodnight," he said softly.

Lisa didn't know what to think. Up to now they were like brother and sister but that kiss was no brotherly kiss. He was just being funny she decided. He always liked to tease her and that was what he was doing now. He said that would be their nightly ritual—a hug and a kiss. Was he teasing or was he serious?

She had to think about this a little. But there was really nothing to think about. Jonathon was Jonathon and he did some strange things. Sitting on the couch eating popcorn and pretending that they were at the movies was fun but it was also rather silly.

Now he was starting something different. Well, she would just go along with him. If he was teasing her as she was sure he was, she'd just act like it was the normal thing for him to do. No way was she going to act surprised.

At any rate, she rather enjoyed the kiss. She could handle a few more like that. She knew that Jonathon always thought of her as a little sister and she thought of him as a big brother. That was okay with her.

Chapter Ten

A Startling Revelation

The next morning she made some coffee and was about to sit down and enjoy a cup when she heard a knock. "Come in, Jonathon," she called.

"I could smell coffee and I need a cup badly."

Lisa poured him a cup and pointed to a chair. "If you like, I'll make some waffles."

"That sounds so good to me."

Pulling out the waffle iron, she quickly plugged it in and then stirred up the waffles batter. In no time they were both eating their breakfast. It had been some time since she had a waffle and it did taste good.

"This is so good. I'd have had to eat old toast or something. Sometimes I don't even eat breakfast but just take a snack with me to the garage. I hate to cook, Lisa. Anytime I can get a meal I didn't have to fix, I take it."

"I'd be glad to cook you breakfast each morning," she volunteered. He sounded almost pitiful.

"Okay."

Lisa looked at him. That was a little too quick an answer. He must have had this planned. Well, she didn't know anyone else's company she enjoyed any more than Jonathon's. She would fix her big brother breakfast every morning but she had to plan what to fix ahead of time.

Soon they heard a cell phone ringing. It was Jonathon's. Someone wanted him to work on their car. He told them he would be there in half an hour.

"Do you want me to come with you and help you?" Lisa asked.

"I'd love to have you come with me, but you don't have to help. It's your day off. I don't want to overwork you."

"You know I love the work."

"All right, come and help me then," Jonathon agreed.

Lisa quickly put the dishes into the sink and walked out the door with Jonathon as they did every day but this day he changed the routine.

He picked up her hand and walked to the car. He seemed almost sad that he had to go to work and she didn't understand that.

"I was planning on taking you for a drive and to the amusement park just for a fun time and now this. I guess business comes first. Maybe next Saturday we can plan something, okay?"

"That would be so nice. I'd like that. Just go out and do something just to have fun for a change. I think it would be good for both of us. But I have fun every day at the garage."

"If it doesn't take too long to fix the car, let's still take the drive and do something fun the rest of the day."

As it was, there wasn't that much wrong with the automobile. It took Jonathon ten minutes to solve the problem. Allan Gaines was pleased. He paid the bill and left a big tip.

So it was about nine o'clock when they went for their drive. They decided they would go to the amusement park and just have a good time. When they arrived they began to pick their rides. Lisa laughed almost all day long and so did Jonathon. He kept hoping that his cell phone wouldn't ring. They ate at some of the food bars on the grounds. Not too bad tasting they decided.

"I like your cooking better," Jonathon remarked.

They stayed the whole day and ate the evening meal there. Lisa couldn't remember a day like this when she had so much fun. Jonathon was always fun to be around in her younger years. Even when he babysat her, he made up fun games for her to play.

They walked around hand in hand. Lisa didn't think too much of it. If he wanted to hold her hand, that was fine.

"Well, I suppose it's about time we started home. We want to get up early in the morning for church." They talked about the great time they had all the way home. When he drove in the driveway, he put his arm around her and hugged her. Then he kissed her again rather passionately. "Remember, that's part of our nightly ritual."

"I remember," she said nervously. "But that sure wasn't a brotherly kiss." She looked at him with questioning eyes.

"I didn't mean it to be a brotherly kiss."

He put his arm around her again and kissed her again and then stepped out of the vehicle. Lisa slipped out of the car and headed for her apartment. It finally dawned on her that Jonathon was serious. These weren't teasing kisses. He loved her. He always did but this was a different type of love.

"Lisa."

She stopped but didn't turn around.

"I love you."

She didn't know what to say. He walked over to her and put his arms around her again.

"I think that you love me too but you haven't admitted it to yourself. You think of me as a big brother but I don't think of you as a little sister. I think of you as someone I want to marry and live with the rest of my life."

"Is that a proposal?"

"It's the best I could do. I love you so much, Lisa, that I don't like being away from you. I want you to think this over. Maybe you don't even love me and I'll have to back off."

"Oh, Jonathon, I've always loved you."

"That's good to hear. It's late tonight but perhaps tomorrow after church we could make some plans."

Lisa nodded her head and walked into her apartment. What just happened? She was proposed to and by telling him she loved him, she agreed to marry him. How did this happen. All this time, she thought Jonathon looked at her as though she was his younger sister. She couldn't believe that he really wanted to marry her. Through the years, she knew he thought of her as a pest, a pitiful kid that needed attention. When did this change come about? When did he start thinking of her as someone he loved and wanted to marry? She had a hard time grasping what just happened.

As she lay down in the bed, she wondered if she would even go to sleep. Oh, Jonathon, I thought you were out of my league. You always thought of me as a pest, a bother, or the grease monkey. And now you want to marry me. How did this happen?

Lisa was happy and thrilled that he had proposed. She wondered how soon Jonathon wanted to get married. What type of wedding would they have? She wanted only a small one. Would he be happy with that? She really would like to wait for a few months but she had an idea that Jonathon might not want to.

Well tomorrow was another day and they would talk about their plans. She was still stunned. How did all this happen so quickly? She thought back to when she was caring for her parents. He never made a move to indicate that he was in love with her. He acted just like the big brother he always was. Maybe he didn't feel free as long as she was tied down with her parents. He sure did help her and her parents and she loved him for that.

She had never thought through the years that Jonathon would think of her as someone to marry. He was her big brother. She was his little sister. Well, evidently not any more.

Chapter Eleven

Trouble at the Garage

Jonathon knocked on Lisa's door and waited for her to answer it. They were going to attend church together. As soon as she opened the door, he hugged her. "I had the best night's sleep just knowing that you're going to marry me. For the last few years I hoped and intended to marry you but I didn't know how you felt about me. I love you," he admitted.

Lisa smiled. He sure looked like a happy man. She had always thought he just wanted to be her big brother so she never let her feelings for him be known. The two drove to the church and entered the building. Several people came over and shook hands with them and welcomed them to the service once again.

They followed along in the song book and sang songs with the rest of the congregation. They enjoyed the song service. When the minister began his sermon they both listened intently. He was a good preacher and they learned a lot that Sunday morning.

After the service, they went to a restaurant. Jonathon held her hand every chance he could or hugged her. When she looked around the restaurant, she saw Sylvia with two women sitting at a table. Sylvia was throwing daggers at her with her eyes. She turned her head and didn't look that way again. She didn't want anything to ruin her dinner. When she went to work tomorrow, what would Sylvia do? Jonathon was treating her like a real date and Sylvia would pick that up. There would be no denying it to the woman tomorrow.

Lisa had such a good time at the meal. The two laughed and talked and stayed at the table for a long time making plans for their marriage.

"You aren't going to make me wait too long before we get married, are you?" Jonathon asked.

"What did you have in mind? I don't want a big wedding, I just want some of our church people but what do you want?" Lisa asked.

"The very same thing," he agreed. "Now, Lisa, I have something for you." He reached in his suit coat and pulled out a box and opened it. There was a beautiful diamond ring. He reached for her left hand and put it on her finger. "Now that makes it official."

Lisa smiled. "Oh, this is so beautiful. I can't believe that I'm going to marry you. I always thought that you thought of me as a little sister. And I thought you were out of my league being so much older than me. But I began to realize that wasn't the case when you kissed me—that wasn't the way a man kisses a sister."

"It wasn't? I didn't know that." Jonathon laughed and Lisa joined him.

"Why don't we wait for one month? That will give you plenty of time to find a dress and anything else you need for the wedding. I'll rent a tuxedo. The Wilson twins would make a flower girl and a ring bearer. What do you think?" he asked.

"That's perfect. I'll get a maid of honor and another girl and you get two guys to stand up with you and that should do it. We'll have to talk with the minister when we get the exact date set. I wonder if we could just have a quick ceremony after church on Sunday morning."

"Let's talk to the minister and find out. Now my future bride, let's go home and rest up for tomorrow. It's another work day tomorrow. I don't want my grease monkey too tired to do her job."

Lisa really laughed. She loved it when he called her that. Sylvia thought it was an insult when he called her grease monkey but she knew better. Jonathon would never insult her or hurt her feelings. Even when she pestered him so much when she was younger, he had patience with her at least most of the time.

When the two returned home they sat in the living room and watched a movie. When the movie was finished, Jonathon kissed her goodnight. Then Lisa went to her apartment. Oh, she could handle a few more of those kisses. She did love Jonathon so much. All these years she held it in but she didn't have to any longer.

The next morning when they arrived at the garage, there were two policemen there waiting for them. Lisa wondered what happened. Did someone break into the garage and take something?

Jonathon frowned and looked at the police and then at Sylvia. "What's the matter, Sergeant Morris? Is something wrong?"

"You mean you don't know? You've been robbed and Sylvia tells me that Lisa Monroe is the thief. You never had any trouble before she came but she's robbed you of Friday's income. I'll be arresting her and taking her down to the station." The officer headed toward Lisa.

"Now wait just one minute. There is no way that Lisa could have robbed the garage. She doesn't even have a key to the garage so she wouldn't be able to get into it to take the money. Just when did you think this robbery occurred, Sylvia? And why do you think Lisa did it?"

"Jonathon, you're so blind and you think you're in love with her that you can't see the truth right in front of you. Now I want her arrested and taken to jail," Sylvia ordered.

Sergeant Morris walked over to Lisa and this time he had the handcuffs out and ready to put on Lisa.

Lisa looked at him and paled.

"Wait just a minute before you do anything, Sergeant Morris. Sylvia you were supposed to bank that money. Why didn't you?"

"I had a date and had to hurry. I didn't think it would hurt to wait until Monday morning to take it to the bank. I never thought that Lisa would steal it. We never had any problems until you hired her."

"Why do you think it was Lisa?" the officer asked.

"Because I followed Lisa and I know exactly what she did with the money. I know where she put it." Sylvia stated it all and seemed so pleased at what she was doing. She was an eye witness to the theft.

"I want to know what time this took place," Jonathon remarked.

"It was nine o'clock last night. I was driving by the garage and noticed her going into the building. I knew she was up to something so

I waited and watched her. She didn't have any idea that I was following her. She placed it in a small hole on the outside of her apartment and put some board against it to hold it in place." Sylvia had the details down flat, she felt.

"At nine o'clock last night, Lisa and I were watching a movie on the television set. I don't know why you're making up this story, but I'm going to have the police arrest you. You were in charge of the money and Lisa had nothing to do with it. She was no where near the garage last night. She went into her apartment at ten thirty. She was with me the rest of the time."

Jonathon looked at the two policemen.

"I think the best thing to do is for us all to go down to the police station and sort this out. Jonathon…"

"Sergeant, there's nothing to sort out, believe me. Somewhere, Sylvia came up with the idea that she was going to marry me. When she saw us yesterday at the restaurant and saw me give Lisa an engagement ring, she made up this whole story to get Lisa in trouble."

The policeman listened carefully to what Jonathon was saying. He had believed the girl and now things didn't look quite so positive against Miss Monroe. However, Jonathon was sure to side in with her if he were engaged to her.

"Now I'm telling you that Lisa had nothing to do with the money and Sylvia had everything to do with it. I suggest you take Sylvia to the place she says the money is hidden and see if it's there. Then get back to me. I need to work today. I have several customers coming and I have two cars that I promised the customer that I'd have ready for them today.

"Take Sylvia to the police station and see if she can pass a lie detector test. Now, take my word, sergeant, Lisa had nothing to do with it. She has no key to get into the garage and she was with me at the time Sylvia accuses her of being at the garage stealing the money."

"She could have had your key copied." Sylvia remarked.

"I have that key with me always and I would have known if she took it."

"Well, mine was missing for a while. She probably copied mine." She stared at Jonathon. This was not turning out the way she thought it would. Now what was she going to do. She knew that Jonathon would fire her. What she should have done was think this thing out thoroughly.

"Come with me, Sylvia, and show me where the money is." The sergeant took her arm and led her to the police car. He was beginning to believe that Jonathon was right. If he was with Lisa all that time, then Sylvia was right out lying. She seemed to have an answer for everything."

"I'm afraid, my little grease monkey, that you'll have to spend a little time in the office today or just keep on eye on the reception area to see if anyone comes in and needs help. I think I know of someone who needs a job and I'll try to get a hold of them. I hope Sylvia doesn't come back and expect to have a job. I hired her because she had no job and she was desperate. I even advanced her money to live on until she had a paycheck. And this is the way she pays me back." Jonathon shook his head.

"Well, let's get to work. I think we'll hear someone come in, but in case we don't hang that big bell on the door. When I worked alone I always hung that on the door so I could hear someone enter the reception area."

Lisa did as he suggested and then went into the garage to help. The whole experience frightened her. Sylvia had told a great story and it appeared that the police believed her and that she was about to be arrested until Jonathon stepped in. Would the police have arrested her on Sylvia's say so if Jonathon hadn't been there to tell them where she had been at nine o'clock?

The police could see her engagement ring and they would weigh carefully anything Jonathon told them about her. They'd probably figure that he was prejudice and he wouldn't even consider her as the thief. But Jonathon knew exactly what was going on. He had seen Sylvia order Lisa around and overheard Sylvia's conversation with Lisa about him already having a girl friend. He didn't say anything because he thought Lisa could work it out. Now he wished he had just fired the girl back then for being so ornery to his neighbor and friend.

Jonathon couldn't help but wonder when the police would return and what they would say. Would they believe him or would they believe Sylvia's wild tale. As he worked away he kept thinking about it. No police showed up all morning.

"Hey, grease monkey, I'm hungry. Can you go pick up two subs and a drink right across the street?" He handed her some money.

"I'll be right back. You sure you're going to get the change back and that I'm not going to steal it from you and never come back to the garage?" she asked teasing.

"Go," he ordered laughing.

It was two in the afternoon when the police showed up. They talked to Lisa first.

"Miss Monroe, you have no record at the police station at all. Sylvia said you did and she thought you had been in prison," Sergeant Morris informed her.

"I've never been in trouble with the police in my life," Lisa assured him. "I certainly haven't been in prison."

"I know. That girl told me so many lies that she kept getting herself mixed up with them. Then she'd tell another lie to try to cover that. But she sure convinced me at first that you were guilty and I was ready to arrest you as soon as you walked in the garage."

"It did seem that way and I wasn't sure what to do. Did she take you to the money?" Jonathon asked.

"It wasn't there. I have an idea that she has it some place. We arrested her but we need you to sign a complaint form."

Jonathon signed the form. "Now you tell Sylvia that she can come for her paycheck but she no longer works here. I've put up with her a little too long because I thought she was in need and I could help her. But she didn't even do the job I assigned her to do."

"She'll have room and board for at least thirty days at the county's expense. It's illegal to file false reports and she knew it was false. Do you have any idea how much money is missing," Sergeant Morris asked.

Jonathon looked over the books and at the bank receipts. He shook his head. "There's no missing money. Sylvia had to make up the whole story up. I was sure she deposited the money Friday after work and this shows that she did. She always leaves a little early on Friday to deposit it."

"How long has she worked for you?" Sergeant Morris asked.

"Almost two years. She was fine until I hired Lisa. I knew she wanted me to date her and become her close friend, but I never could do that. But in her mind, she felt that one day I'd marry her. She was sure jealous of Lisa. Sylvia sure gave my fiancé a bad time ordering her around and demanding she do the job Sylvia was supposed to do," Jonathon explained.

The policeman changed the subject. He had heard about all he wanted to about Sylvia. When he spent that time with her looking for the money, she got under his skin. So he turned to Lisa and picked up her hand. "That's a beautiful ring on your finger, Lisa."

"It sure is," Lisa agreed.

"We're making plans to get married soon. I've known this young lady long enough to know what a sweet gal she is," Jonathon remarked.

"I offer my congratulations to both of you."

"Thank you," they both stated in unison.

The policeman left. He was sure pleased that Jonathon had stepped in and corrected him before he arrested Lisa. With the look on Lisa's face when he walked over to arrest her, he knew something was wrong. She wasn't trying to get away she was frightened and didn't know what to do.

Now he would have to deal with Sylvia while she was held in prison. Maybe he could pull rank and turn her over to some other policeman. He was in no mood to deal with her now.

If he charged her for every lie that she told him, she would never get out of prison. What he couldn't figure out was, if Sylvia was making a charge against Lisa, why didn't she hide the money where it couldn't be found.

Evidently when it came to framing someone, Sylvia's mentality wasn't all that great.

Chapter Twelve

Jacob Brown's Problem

After the policeman left, the two went right to work. "Jonathon, if it's just receiving the customers and asking them what they need done with their vehicles, why couldn't I do that in between helping you? I could take their money, checks or credit card payments. If that's all there is to do, you wouldn't need to hire someone else."

"We'll do that for a while but you're so much help as my grease monkey that I can't spare you too much time for the office. We'll see how it works out. Oh, oh, there's your first call. I hear the bell ringing."

Lisa walked out into the reception room. "Hello, how may I help you?" she asked the elderly man.

"My car doesn't sound right. I'd like Jonathon to take a look at it. Now my daughter drove me down here so please have him call me and let me know how much it will cost to have it fixed and call me when it's fixed." He handed the key to Lisa and she walked outside and looked at the automobile. Boy that was an old one. She wondered if Jonathon had worked on one like that before. It looked like a 1930 or 1940 vehicle. It would be fun to see what that vehicle's engine looked like.

"We'll give you a call. Now let me get your name, address and phone number. Just fill this out." Lisa waited until the man was through. His name was Harvey Matthews. She would try to remember that. She liked it when people remembered her name so she hoped she could remember the names of all the customers as they came into the reception area.

"Thank you, Mr. Matthews. We'll be in touch with you."

Mr. Matthews nodded and looked at Lisa. "You tell Jonathon that he sure has a better looking secretary today than he did have before," he remarked and headed for his daughter's vehicle. He waved goodbye to Lisa.

"What a nice man," she thought. But so far most of the customers had been nice and not demanding. Jonathon had some good people that came in for their vehicle repairs. That made it all the nicer to work in his garage.

She barely stepped into the garage when she heard the bell ring again. She so wanted to work on an automobile but she went to greet the customer. When she saw the boy walk through the door, she knew who he was because he went to her church each Sunday.

"Hello, Lisa. You remember me, I know. I'm Jacob Brown. I've been all over town looking for a job. My dad was laid off from work because they downsized the company. Is there any chance you might have some job around here so I could get a little money to take home. I'll be glad to do anything that needs to be done. I'm not a bad mechanic either."

"I think you came at a good time, Jacob. You stay right here and let me talk with Jonathon." Lisa hurried into the garage.

"Jonathon, Mr. Matthews brought his car in. Have you seen it before?"

"Oh, yes. Older than the hills that vehicle is. He probably had his daughter drive him here so I don't have to be in a hurry. I sure need your help."

"Jacob Brown is looking for a job because his father's work place down sized and he lost his job. Could we hire him for the receptionist and I'll show him what to do. It sounds so simple."

"Be my guest. I'd like to help the Browns as they are nice people and I think they have three children. I've watched the family at church and the children are well behaved. Go train Jacob."

Lisa walked back to the reception area and smiled at Jacob. "You have a job. Now here's your desk. What you'll do is greet the people who come in the reception room and see what they want. You'll have them fill out this paper so we know who they are along with their address and phone number. They need to list the problem they are having with their car. If they wish to speak to Jonathon, you can walk into the garage and let him know that a customer wants to talk with him.

"When you have everything done and have the area cleaned you can check with me. I'm sure there's plenty of work to keep you busy."

"That sounds simple. I can handle that," Jacob remarked enthusiastically. He had a job. He didn't have any idea how much money he would be paid but anything would help his family. He was excited. Just maybe when he didn't have anything to do in the reception area, they might let him work on a car. He could only hope.

"Now this is an employee form so you need to fill that out when there is no one here. You're seventeen, right?"

"That's right. Thanks for the job, Lisa. You can't imagine how much I needed some work. We're getting desperate."

"I know how that feels," Lisa remarked. "You can thank Jonathon for the job when you see him."

She headed for the garage and began to work on a vehicle that was supposed to be done this very day. Jonathon had shown her how to use the computer diagnostic system for the newer cars and how to tell what was wrong with the vehicle. She loved doing that. The car was a newer one so she hooked it up to the machine and let it run through the loops to find the problem. It appeared that a fuse was burned out.

Lisa found the correct fuse and removed everything that she needed to get to the proper place. She inserted the fuse and then worked on putting everything back in the proper place. She started the car and it ran smoothly. A smile crept across her face and Jonathon looked at her about that time.

"Pretty proud of yourself, aren't you?" he asked.

"I love this work. I know most girls don't but I love it. Now I'll check on our receptionist and see how he is doing. I heard the bell ring twice."

When Lisa walked into the room, she saw two men filling out paperwork. Jacob was asking them when they needed their car. One of them said in about two days and the other one wanted it today if at all possible. Jacob promised the gentleman that he'd see what he could do.

"Let me take a look at the car that needs done today. That's for Pierce Lowry," Lisa suggested. She looked outside at the car. Not brand new but not too old. She drove it into the bay. He said the brakes weren't working right. This was something new to Lisa but she remembered reading about how to replace the breaks.

Since she had never done this before, she had written herself some notes. She carefully followed the notes and discovered the brake bands were worn down and needed replacing, but the drums were still okay. She checked and found that Jonathon had bands in stock so she replaced them.

Jonathon had finished the repairs on his automobile and he was carefully watching her to see if she did it right. He knew this was the first time she had changed brakes. "How did you know how to do that?" he asked.

"That book you gave me. I've been studying it and I made notes on how to replace the brakes. Did you want to see if I did them right?" she asked.

"Listen, my little grease monkey, I have been watching you do it and you did it perfect. You're such a good helper. He put his arm around her and kissed her.

"Is that the proper thing to do in the work place," she asked.

"Since I know the owner, I think it's alright," Jonathon laughed.

Lisa drove the car out and went back to Jacob. "Did you have a phone number for the man who wanted his car right away?"

"Yes, I do."

"Call him and tell him it is ready."

Jacob made the call. No one else came in and he stepped into the garage. "Is there any possibility when there's nothing to do out there that I might learn to do a few things in here?"

Jonathon looked at him and smiled. "Have you ever worked on cars?"

"Yes, I have an old clunker. I change the oil myself, fix the breaks and about anything else on the car. I can't afford to take it to a mechanic."

"Well, there is a car that need the oil change, a filter, and then cleaned. Go to it," Jonathon suggested.

Jacob smiled. While he was in the middle of the job, the bell rang.

"Finish your job, Jacob. I'll see to this customer," Jonathon ordered and walked into the reception area. He had several cars to fix so he was going to enjoy Jacob's help when he wasn't at the desk.

"Hi, Donald, what can I do for you?"

"My car is in terrible shape and I know you're going to want to keep it for a week. I had to have it towed in here. I'll just have to take the bus to work. I should have brought it in when it first acted up. There's something wrong with the engine and I think it needs brakes and the steering wheel isn't working right. Do what you can when you can and call me when it's finished." Donald finished filling out the paper work and left. The man looked a little upset as he walked away from the garage.

When he went into the garage, he noticed that Jacob had finished with the vehicle he was working on and drove it out of the bay placing the number in the window. He was coming back in looking at another car and saw what it needed and went right to work on it. Jonathon thought he would just let him work in the garage for a while. One look at the young man and he knew he was enjoying himself. He didn't ask any questions on how to do repairs. He knew what he was doing.

Jonathon decided that he could use a cup of coffee and relax for a minute or two. He had felt under pressure with so many vehicles to be repaired but his crew of two was going through them quickly.

Jonathon looked into the garage and saw Jacob looking at another car. "If you know how to fix that one, Jacob, be my guest."

Jacob smiled and started in on it.

Lisa had finished two cars and they were waiting for their owners. Jonathan had a cup of coffee and sat down. He had worked hard and now he could take a break. It looked as if he was going to get completely caught up with Jacob's help. Then he had an idea. He would let Jacob fix Donald's car. If he could fix that he could fix anything.

Lisa came out and saw him sitting having a cup of coffee. "Is it break time or something?" she asked.

"Well, my two workers were doing such a good job that I thought I would just take a break."

"Jacob is a good mechanic, Jonathon. Did you watch him working? He knows a lot more about repairing automobiles than I do. I think you should keep him in the garage and I'll watch the reception area," she suggested reluctantly.

"Yes, I did watch him and I'm impressed. We're going to get caught up on all those automobiles that need to be repaired. That makes me feel good. I wonder if Jacob needs to be paid tonight. Would you talk to him and see if he needs money now? He sounded pretty desperate when I talk with him," Jonathon remarked. He liked Jacob and was pleased that he had come to the garage at the right time.

"Will do as soon as I have my coffee break," she replied.

"Oh, I didn't think grease monkeys got coffee breaks."

Lisa ignored him and filled her cup with coffee. Then she headed in to talk with Jacob.

"How long has your dad been out of work?" she asked.

"For three weeks and he just can't find any work in his line. He keeps trying and he does get some unemployment checks and that helps but it isn't enough to feed the family and pay the house payment."

"Do you need some money tonight?" she asked.

"That would be a big relief. I could get some groceries for my mom if I had a little money. Dad took most of his unemployment check to pay the house payment. There wasn't much left over for food."

Jonathon looked over the bay. He had two empty bays. That was good. "Jacob, it's almost quitting time. Donald brought in his car and there are several things wrong with it. I'm turning that over to you. Tomorrow you work on his vehicle."

Jacob was all smiles. "Thanks, I'll do that. I'm like Lisa as I love to work on automobiles no matter what's wrong with them."

"Well, clean up and stop at the desk and I'll give you today's pay. Now you let me know when you need some more money. It doesn't matter if I pay you every day or every week. You do good work and you have a job. But what about when school starts what will you do?"

"I thought I'd either home school or try to go to school at night. I just have one more year and I'll graduate. I sure would like to finish but I wouldn't want to lose this job. I've always wanted to work in a garage repairing automobiles. It was my dream to become an automobile mechanic and that's what I'm doing now."

"We'll work something out, Jacob."

He wrote out a check for Jacob and handed it to him.

"Jonathon, that's a lot of money for one day," he exclaimed with a surprise look on his face. He thought perhaps his new boss made a mistake.

"You're a good mechanic and you earned every bit of it. Now I'll see you at eight o'clock in the morning. The grocery store on the corner will gladly cash that check for you if you intend to get some groceries. They always take my checks."

Jacob went home happy. He could hardly wait to tell his family that he not only had a job but he had a job that he had one that he always wanted.

Chapter Thirteen

The Accident

On the way home, Jonathon suggested that Lisa had hired a mechanic instead of a receptionist and therefore she still had to handle the customers as they came in. He hoped she wasn't too disappointed.

Lisa stared at him but smiled. "I know that Jacob is a better mechanic than I am and I don't mind doing the reception work as long as I get to work on the cars now and then. Okay?" she asked.

"Well, I thought maybe all three of us could take turns. How would that be?"

"Perfect," Lisa answered.

For the next two weeks, they were able to keep up with all the cars that came into the garage. No one had to wait too long to get their automobile back. Jonathon was pleased how things were working out. He didn't work as hard as he used to. With Lisa and Jacob both working on the vehicles everything was getting done and people were getting their vehicles back in a very timely manner.

One morning at work, Jonathon remembered that he was out of an item that he needed and he knew that he could purchase the item at the local auto supply store across town. Usually he kept a good supply of repair items in his garage but he had missed that one. "Lisa, I have to go over to the supply store and pick up some repair parts. Take care of the garage while I'm gone. I should be back within the hour."

"Will do, boss" she answered.

She and Jacob worked on the vehicles. Lisa took care of the customers that come in and let Jacob stay in the garage. He knew a lot more than she did and sometimes she enjoyed talking to the customers. She had an idea that Jacob didn't. He was a little backward when it came to meeting people but he sure wasn't when it came to repairing a vehicle.

It was noon time and Jonathon wasn't back. He told her he would be back in an hour. "Jacob, did you bring a lunch?"

"Yes, I did and I'm getting hungry. I'm at a good stopping place so I'm taking my lunch break."

"I'm going to get me a sub across the street. Watch the reception area until I get back."

Lisa was back in no time. After she ate, she decided to call Jonathon's cell phone. She let it ring several times and finally a woman said hello. "Isn't this Jonathon Livingston's cell phone," she asked.

"Yes, it is. He was in an accident and he's in the hospital. Are you a friend of his?" she asked.

"Yes, I'm his fiancé. I'll come right down there." Lisa had tears in her eyes as she hung up the phone.

"What's wrong, Lisa?"

"Jonathon's had an accident and he's in the hospital. Can you answer the door and work on the cars both while I go check on him?"

"Sure I can. You go. Let's just pray that it isn't anything serious." Jacob suggested. He sure hoped his friend wasn't hurt too badly. He sure enjoyed visiting with Jonathon while they worked on the automobiles.

"They didn't give me any details. I'll be back as soon as I can," Lisa promised. She had no idea what she would find when she reached the hospital.

Lisa hurried out to one of the spare cars that Jonathon kept at his work site. He was always buying old clunkers and fixing them up. She drove to the hospital a little faster than the speed limit allowed. Once there she hurried to the information desk to find out which room Jonathon was in.

"Miss, we can't give out any information until we notify the family first," the nurse informed her.

"I'm the only family he has. I'm his fiancé. Now please let me see him," Lisa begged.

"I'll call the doctor and see if he is out of surgery yet."

"Out of surgery? It was bad enough that he had to have surgery? Please tell me everything."

"A drunk driver hit his car. His back is in bad shape and the doctor doesn't know if he'll ever walk again. Now, let me call the doctor and see how soon they'll finish the surgery and put him in a room where you can see him." The nurse called and finally said thank you.

"He's out of surgery and in room 110. You may go see him but he'll be a little drowsy. He may not make a lot of sense when you talk to him."

Lisa hurried down the hall to Jonathon's room. As she walked in she looked at him. He was awake and staring at the ceiling. "Jonathon, darling, are you all right? Are you awake?"

Jonathon looked at her. "I'm so glad that you came, sweetheart. I suppose Jacob is watching the garage."

"Yes, and he's doing a good job. You don't have to worry about that garage, Jacob and I will take care of it. How do you feel? You know we're going to get married in two weeks. You have to be well by that time," Lisa remarked and smiled at him. She kissed his cheek.

"Lisa, I'm not going to get married until I can walk. The doctors aren't sure when that will be. I'm not going to burden you with a crippled husband."

As she looked at Jonathon, she knew he meant that. What should she say? "Darling, you're going to walk as soon as you heal up a little. I know you. You can't accept that you won't be able to walk and you'll just get up and do it to show the doctors," Lisa stated.

Jonathon laughed. "You know me a little too well. They say I shouldn't feel any pain in my legs and they don't believe me when I tell them I can. I'm going to walk again so please be patient with me, darling. We don't have to be in a hurry to get married. I don't want to go down the aisle in a wheel chair. I hope you understand my feelings about that."

"I do, Jonathon. I can't blame you for not wanting to go down the aisle as a crippled man. Have they told you when you can get out of here?" she asked.

"They said by Monday I could go home. I need a ramp put on the back door so I can get into the house with my wheel chair. Could you get a carpenter to put one there? I don't know what I'm going to do with the garage."

"Don't you worry one minute about the garage and the automobiles at the garage. Jacob and I will take care of that. I think you should come and be the receptionist when you're feeling better."

"You little grease monkey. You always wanted me to be the receptionist and you'd be the mechanic. But you're right. That's about all I'll be good for at least for a while. This is Friday so we'll see what Monday brings. Outside of my legs, I feel pretty good. They won't let me even try to sit up until tomorrow. After you close the shop today, please come back and be with me," Jonathon pleaded.

Jonathon sounded so pitiful. It wasn't like him at all. She knew he hated to lie around and to lie around in a hospital was even worse for him. "I'll be here until they throw me out or ask me to leave," she promised and smiled at him. She bent and kissed the man she loved.

"Oh, that's what I missed. One more kiss, please."

"Now what are you doing to my patient. You're getting him all upset. Look, his blood pressure is going up. You can't go around kissing patients in the hospital," the doctor stated and laughed.

"Can you tell me how he is? Will he get to go home Monday? When can he try to walk? Is he going to be okay?"

"Hold on, that's a lot of questions. I believe he'll be able to go home Monday but in a wheel chair. He does need to follow up with Dr. Jensen. Now he needs a van with a ramp so he can roll his wheel chair in the van and you can drive him home. He'll need another ramp at the house. Both of these ramps can be rented and that's what I'd suggest you do. Jonathon tells me that he's going to walk again so you don't want something for a long term. He claims he can feel some pain in his legs. If he can, that's good but I don't see how he can with the damage that was done." The doctor shook his head.

"Dr. Simmons, can I try to sit up some?" Jonathon asked. He was so tired just lying on his back. If he could change positions it would help a little. It was going to be a long time between now and Monday when he would get to go home.

"If you think you're ready. You sure came out of the surgery and woke up fast. You're a very healthy man." The doctor helped him to sit up. Then he lifted the blanket. You tell me when I touch your leg.

"Now you're touching my knees," Jonathon remarked.

The doctor was shocked. "You're right but I don't see how you can feel anything. After the damage was done, you need to heal before you can feel anything. I don't understand it." The doctor shook his head again.

"Doc, I have another doctor looking out for me. He's God and He's going to get me through this. I have a garage to take care. This little grease monkey here works for me and she's going to have to run the shop until I get well."

"She's your grease monkey? I thought she was your fiancée."

"She's both."

"When's the wedding?"

"It was supposed to be in two weeks, but I'm going to wait until I can walk. I want to be standing up when I marry my bride. I don't want to be in a wheel chair," Jonathon stated firmly.

"Jonathon, I believe you'll walk with the determination you have. Perhaps tomorrow you can give it a try. But please don't try today. Give the surgery a little time first. Now you seem comfortable sitting up so you can do that. I'll see you before I go home today."

"I should go check on Jacob and the garage and make sure he isn't overwhelmed with work. He sure is a good mechanic, Jonathon." Lisa made the remark and watched Jonathon's reaction.

"Yes he is and you go and see what you can do to help him but please come back after work."

"I promise," she stated and kissed him.

Lisa hated to leave but someone had to take care of the garage and it was unfair to Jacob to leave him alone so she hurried out of the hospital and drove to the garage. When she entered the reception area, Jacob had three men in there filling out paper work. He told them that they could call him tomorrow and he would let them know if their vehicles were ready. They didn't seem upset over that. He had explained that Jonathon had an accident so it would take a little longer to repair the vehicles than usual. Jacob apologized.

When they left, Lisa asked him how things went.

"Well, I've finished three cars and two of the people came and picked them up. I wrote paid on their slip and put the amount in the ledger. I tried to do the bookwork as it looked like you've been doing. You better check and make sure I did it right. It seems like a simple way of keeping books."

Lisa looked at the ledger. "You did just as you were supposed to. You have the time it took you and the amount of oil or fuses or whatever you used. You did a good job and I didn't even have to teach you. Now, why don't we take care of a few of those cars before we go home?"

"How is Jonathon?" Jacob asked.

"The doctor didn't think he would walk again, but he can already feel his legs. I think he'll be walking long before the doctor thinks he will. He's a strong man and a determined one."

The two cleared the bays and only had two cars left by the time they closed the shop. It was a little later than they usually quit but they didn't want too many vehicles lined up to be repaired. Jacob headed home but Lisa grabbed a sub and headed for the hospital.

What if Jonathon never did walk as the doctor thought? No, she wasn't going to think that. She had purchased her wedding dress and every thing she needed for the wedding. They had planned a simple church wedding but he wasn't willing to go through with it until he could walk. She hated putting off the wedding but in a way, she couldn't blame Jonathon to want to wait until he could walk down the aisle instead of wheeling down it.

When she arrived at the hospital and stepped in Jonathon's room, he welcomed her with a big smile. He held out his arms for a hug and she walked over and hugged him. It was good to get that hug. She missed him when he was away from her.

"Lisa, I can move my legs. Look at this," he exclaimed and moved his leg pushing the blanket up quite a ways.

"Jonathon, you're going to walk long before that doctor thinks you are. What did the doctor say when you showed him?"

"He just shook his head. He couldn't believe it. I think God is helping me. Now tell me how the garage did today."

"You're not going to believe this, boss, but we cleared out all but two cars. Jacob didn't work on the clunker as he felt that the other cars were in a bigger rush to be finished according to their owners."

"He's a wise young man. I'm pleased that he came to work for us. I don't know what we would have done without him if this accident had happened before we hired him. Thank the Lord for special favors."

"Today, while I was at the hospital, he took care of several things in the office and posted things right and I hadn't even shown him how to do some of it. He just looked at the books and figured it out himself."

"Well, it looks as if I can just stay in the hospital and enjoy my vacation and rake in the money."

Lisa just shook her head. She knew that Jonathon wanted to get out of that hospital and fast. This was definitely not a vacation to him. He was already restless but he was looking forward to Monday. It couldn't come too soon to please him.

"Are you going to let Jacob take care of any automobiles tomorrow?" Jonathon asked.

"He said he wanted to go in and work on the clunker. That way if anyone else comes in he can see if they are in a hurry or not. I thought that sounded like a good idea. He told me to visit with you and he would listen for the bell in case someone came in the reception area."

"I think he would stay there all night if we let him. He does love the job."

They heard someone step into the room and looked up to see the nurse frowning. "I think it's about time you let my patient rest. It's late," she informed Lisa.

Lisa hadn't paid any attention to the time. She was just enjoying visiting with Jonathon. She kissed him goodbye and left. She supposed ten o'clock was a little late to keep the patient awake.

Chapter Fourteen

Recovery Time

Monday evening, Lisa wheeled Jonathon out of the hospital and into the van with the loading ramp. She drove him home and carefully helped him wheel the chair down the ramp. They finally made it into the house and he relaxed. He hadn't been home too long before there was a knock on the door.

Lisa answered the knock. "Hello, can I help you?" she asked.

"I'm James Addison. I'm a lawyer and I need to talk with Jonathon Livingston about his vehicle accident.

Lisa invited the man in and led him into the living room where Jonathon was sitting.

"Hello, Jonathon. I hope you're doing okay. It appeared the man who ran into your car is quite wealthy and as your lawyer I want to make sure you get a good settlement. After what that drunk driver did to you, you deserve a good size settlement."

"Whatever you think, James. I don't know much about law suits but I feel I'm entitled to something for the pain and the loss of work. You do what you think you should."

Jonathon hated suing anyone but at the same time, the man shouldn't have been driving while he was drunk. It evidently wasn't the first time. He wasn't going to worry about anything and he'd just let the lawyer handle it. Jonathon wondered if he was going to make enough money in the garage to pay his two workers. He would wait until tomorrow and have Lisa take him to the garage. He felt good but he just couldn't walk as yet.

Jonathon shook hands with James and said goodbye. "Just let me know what you find out," he asked.

"I'll be seeing you. It may take two or three months but you'll get a good settlement, I promise you." With that said, the lawyer left.

"Jonathon, I know you don't like the idea of suing someone, but it is only right that you do. The man has to be stopped from hitting other people and crippling them. This might be his wakeup call," Lisa remarked.

"I know you're right. I'm just turning it all over to the lawyer and I'm not going to worry about it until he places a check in my hands."

"That a good plan," Lisa agreed.

Tuesday, Jonathon wheeled into the garage and looked over the books. He was shocked at the number of cars his two workers had repaired. He had a list at the cost per hour and per job. The two helpers followed it exactly. He wasn't pleased that he couldn't help repair vehicles but he relaxed knowing everything was working out great without his help. He had an idea that Jacob probably put in a little overtime to get that many cars serviced. He had given the young man a key to the garage and he suspected that he worked late at night and on Saturday. Well, he'd make his paycheck a little more than usual.

He played the receptionist for the next week. Lisa helped him to stand now and then. Jacob on one side and with Lisa on the other, he even took a few steps. He didn't want to over do it as the doctor had warned him not to. If he did he'd never walk, the doctor told him. Each day that following week, he took a few more steps. He wasn't ready to work on cars as yet even though he could do a little walking. He knew that once he got down on the floor and crawled under a car, he probably would never be able to get up again.

No, he wouldn't do that. Those two were taking good care of the cars that needed to be repaired. Jacob was always pleased with his paycheck but Lisa didn't want to take one.

"Until we're married, you'll take a pay check," he informed her and stared right at her as if that were a command and she better obey it.

"You can stand up now so we could get married," she teased.

"I want to be doing a little better. Let's make it two months from now. I know we're both disappointed but it's not fair to you to be stuck with a cripple. In two months I should be doing well and should be able to repair cars again." He kissed her as he could see the disappointment on her face.

It was past the date that they first set for their wedding. Now she had to wait for another two months. But she tried to tell herself what a great thing it was that she would have Jonathon for a husband eventually. There wasn't any one like him. He was the best. She had dated only a few times before her parents became ill. But she never dated anyone that she wanted to spend the rest of her life with—only Jonathon fit that bill. He was worth waiting for. Lisa had an idea that her parents would have been very pleased that she was going to marry Jonathon. They really liked the young man.

For the next month, Jonathon took care of the books and the reception area. He walked now and then but not too far. He felt that each day he gained a little more strength than he had the day before.

In one month he and Lisa were to be married. He wanted to make sure he had all his strength by then and was walking easily. He didn't want to stick his beautiful finance with a handicapped man.

At least she didn't have to wheel him into the house or to the garage anymore. He tried not to overdo it as the doctor had warned him but it was hard. He often went into the garage and watched the two mechanics repair the vehicles. Lisa was having the time of her life. He knew she wouldn't want to go back to the reception desk when he was well but he would allow her to work on the cars sometimes.

Jonathon only used the wheelchair when he had to walk a long ways which he seldom did. He was ready to donate it to someone who really needed it. At his last doctor's appointment, he was informed that he was doing excellent and in another two months he'd be back in the shape he was before the accident. The doctor was very pleased at his progress and the fact that he followed his orders. Not all of his patients did.

When he thought what the doctor said, he'd like to wait two more months before he married but he wasn't sure how Lisa would take that. He postponed the first date and now if he postponed the second date, she would begin to think he didn't want to get married and that wasn't true. He just wanted to be in good shape when he did.

Lisa was out in the reception area having a cup of coffee and Jacob was just coming out of the garage when a man entered the building.

"Tell me, sweetie, would you like to place an ad in the newspaper for the garage and get more customers?" the man asked looking right at Lisa and smiling a big smile and he laughed slightly.

"Jacob, he must be talking to you because my name isn't sweetie." Lisa turned and went back into the garage.

"Well, I'm not sweetie either so he must be talking to you, Jonathon," Jacob remarked and followed Lisa into the garage. They decided to drink their coffee somewhere they would be free of that man. Jacob wanted to laugh at Lisa's reactions but then thought better of it.

"My name's sure not sweetie either," Jonathon explained and turned and stared at the man with less than a pleasant face.

"I'm sorry I didn't know the young lady would resent that so much. Some girls like to be called that," he remarked and apologized.

"Not my fiancé. She only likes me to call her that." Jonathon's voice was very unfriendly.

"Would you be interested in placing an ad in the newspaper?"

"Actually we have all the work we need. If things ever change, I'll call the newspaper. But I've had the garage for years and people seemed to like my work and they come back to my garage when they have any car trouble. The even recommend it to their friends."

"Oh. Well thank you anyway," the man remarked and left. He had started that conversation all wrong and he had an idea that even if the garage owner needed an ad he wouldn't call him and give him the business. Next time he'd use a little better judgment when he first met potential clients. One lesson learned and he was going to remember it.

Jonathon went into the garage. "Sweetie, you can come out now."

Lisa glared at him.

Jacob and Jonathon laughed a little too hard to suit Lisa.

Jonathon smacked himself on his forehead and turned to Jacob. "I just thought of something. Lisa and I should put our wedding announcement in the paper. Maybe I should call Sweetie back."

Jacob looked real thoughtful and replied, "Maybe it should read: 'Granger Garage Boss to marry Grease Monkey soon."

When Jonathon noticed the look on Lisa's face, he said, "Oops. What I meant to say was Lisa you can come out now, Sweetie just left," Jonathon stated and laughed some more along with Jacob.

It was as if the two had the giggles like silly little girls, Lisa thought. "You two aren't near as funny as you think you are." The idea of that newspaper man calling her sweetie when she had never seen him before in her life was disgusting. She was fuming for a few minutes and then decided to forget the whole thing.

"I don't think he'll be coming back. You're safe to get another cup of coffee when you need one, sweetheart." He stressed the sweetheart. He knew how far to push her and if he called her sweetie he knew he'd be in hot water. It was fun to tease Lisa but he never wanted to hurt her feelings.

That evening, Jonathon drove home. It was the first time since his accident. He wanted to start doing things and get back to normal. He was feeling pretty good now but he'd follow the doctor's orders and not over do.

"In one month, we're getting married. We're still just going to have a few people and go to the church and have the minister do the ceremony, isn't that right, Jonathon? That's still our plans?"

"The pastor talked to me Sunday and he seems to think we should let the whole church come and they'd provide the dinner after the ceremony. He suggested we have it after the morning service. I told him I'd talk with you. Sometimes, I think he's right. If people know we're getting married and exclude them from coming, how are they going to feel toward us?"

"He talked to me too. Okay, let's let him have his way. I have my dress and veil and I'm all ready. You have a nice suit or were you going to get a tuxedo?"

"No, I'm just going to wear a suit. We need two witnesses so I'll have Jacob as my best man and you need to select a friend for maid of honor."

"I wonder if Jacob's sister would be my maid of honor. I'll ask him. We went a few places together before my parents fell ill. I'll ask him to see what she says or perhaps I'll call her. Now we're not going to take a honeymoon trip at this time, are we? We're so busy I don't see how we can get away from the garage."

"Let's wait for a while. I agree that we're too busy now. I thought that I might hire Jacob's dad. Jacob said he was an excellent mechanic. He was working as a bookkeeper for a company that downsized him out of a job. But Jacob said he liked being a mechanic better. Lisa, we've really raked in the money the last few months with you and Jacob working. I can afford to hire another man and after he is good and trained, we could take our honeymoon." Jonathon didn't want to disappoint her but she seemed to understand that one day they would take their honeymoon but not right after the marriage.

"That sounds like a good plan. Jacob's family is so proud of him and so pleased with the money he brings home. He's going to home school his last year and one of the teachers is going to help him. Since he wants to be a mechanic anyway that sounded like a good idea."

Jonathon asked Jacob to talk with his father and see if he was interested. With all these mechanics, he was going to have to enlarge his garage.

Jacob told his dad that Jonathon wanted another mechanic. Joseph Brown was pleased. He would go to the garage the very next day with Jacob and talk to Jonathon. He was excited. While the bookkeeping job was okay, it wasn't what he wanted to do. It happened to be the only job he could find at the time. He had studied bookkeeping in college so he qualified for that job. But he hoped it wouldn't last a life time.

Joseph had listened to his son talked about the garage and about Lisa and Jonathon. He always came home so happy and pleased with his job. He knew Jacob was doing exactly what he wanted to do and he was doing a good job. Almost every Sunday Jonathon would stop and talk to Joseph about how well his son was doing.

"I've never found a vehicle I couldn't repair, yet," Jacob informed his dad smiling that smile that only Jacob smiled.

Joseph was shocked at the large amount of pay that his son was receiving but then mechanics did make good wages. He guessed he considered his son a child and they weren't supposed to make that much money. But Jacob wasn't a child now. He would soon be eighteen and he was a man. Right now Jacob was the bread supplier for the family. Joseph's unemployment checks paid the house payment and utilities while Jacob's checks bought the food and everything else that was needed.

Jacob told him that he was going to be Jonathon's best man at his and Lisa's wedding.

His father was surprised. "How did he happen to pick you?"

"Dad, we've become real good friends. When I applied for the job, Jonathon was really in need of someone. They were going to make me the receptionist but when I ran out of work and started repairing cars, they never mentioned receptionist again. I think Jonathon was shocked to see I knew so much about cars. Through the years you had taught me a lot about vehicle repair and then I took auto mechanics in high school and learned a lot."

"You did him a good job, son. Evidently, you don't goof around. You work just like I taught you to. I'm proud of you and I'm rather excited about having a chance to get to be a mechanic again."

Chapter Fifteen

Jacob's Father

When Jonathon arrived at home that evening, he checked his mailbox. He glanced through all of the ads and miscellaneous mail before he found an interesting letter. He studied it carefully. It appeared to be from his attorney. It must be something about his accident. After opening the letter and reading it, he knocked on Lisa's door.

"Lisa, look at this letter and tell me what you think?" Jonathon said watching for her reaction. Lisa opened the door for him to come in. She was cooking their dinner in her apartment as she had the crock pot simmering. She often started the food cooking and had it shut off at a certain time and that way she could eat shortly after she returned home.

She took the letter and looked it over. It was the settlement for Jonathon's accident if he accepted it. "If you don't accept this offer, it will likely be years before you even get a settlement. I know you deserve more, but $300,000 is a lot of money, Jonathon. And the company will pay your doctor bills associated with your accident. Anything that has to do with your accident whether it is a doctor bill or a stay in the hospital will be paid by the man's insurance company." That was what his lawyer had written.

"I think you should accept this offer. If you wait too long you might get nothing or less," Lisa remarked.

"That's what I think, darling. I own the land on both sides of the garage and in back. What if I were to enlarge the garage?" he asked her.

"What a good idea, but let's get married first."

"Why did I know you were going to say that?" Jonathon asked with a smile.

So Jonathon decided to accept the check. That money would do a lot to enlarge the garage and buy more equipment that he'd need for an extra mechanic. He would bank it in the morning.

The next morning he remembered that Jacob's father would likely be at the garage shortly after he arrived. Lisa and Jonathon always arrived at the garage a half hour ahead of time to turn on the heat and see what needed to be done for the day. It wasn't long before Joseph Brown drove up and walked into the garage.

"My son tells me that you're looking for another mechanic. I'm the one that taught him what he knows. He sure took to it and learned quickly. We had purchased an old car and together we got it running."

"He does a great job and if you want to work here, you're hired. Now I wonder if you're any kind of a builder. I'm going to enlarge the garage so we have more bays. You ever do much building?"

"I built our home so the answer is yes. You have to get your plan laid out and approved by the city and then we can start in," Joseph remarked.

Jonathon liked him right off. He seemed like a go getter. "I guess I don't have to introduce you to Lisa since you've seen her at church. She's a mechanic as well and mind you, she's a good one."

"That's what Jacob said. I hear you two are getting married shortly. Congratulations."

"Since you were a bookkeeper, I may have you do our books. That's something I don't like. It shouldn't take up too much of your time. The bookkeeping system is very simple. I hope you don't mind."

"I'll be your carpenter, your bookkeeper and your mechanic. Is there anything else?" he asked and smiled. Most people didn't like to do bookkeeping as one mistake was often hard to find. But he was good at it and didn't mind doing that type of work but preferred to be a mechanic.

Jonathon laughed. "We're going to get along great."

Joseph headed for the garage and looked at the first vehicle and took the paper to see what the problem was. He grabbed a pair of coverall and went right to work. Lisa finished her job, drove the car out of the bay and parked it and went into the reception room.

"Mr. Brown is a happy man. He appears to be enjoying himself. After not working for a while, this is great for him. I heard him say he was a carpenter and you asked him to be the bookkeeper. That was one job I didn't care too much for but I didn't mind doing it."

"I know, grease monkey, you just want to work on the cars." Jonathon hugged her. They both had another cup of coffee and relaxed.

Lisa was just about ready to go outside and drive the next car into one of the open bays when a man walked into the garage. She waited a minute to see what was going on.

"We're selling insurance policies," the rough-faced man remarked in not too friendly voice.

"We already have an insurance agency, but thank you," Jonathon informed him and turned back to his work.

"This is a different type of insurance. This will keep your place free from people breaking into your garage at night or starting a fire or bombing the place." The man stared at him as if he dared him not to accept the offer.

"We've never had any trouble of that type so I'm not interested" Jonathon said emphatically. What was this man trying to pull? Evidently he was from some gang and Jonathon wasn't about to be intimidated with him.

"The cost is only ten percent of your profits. Now that's not much money for us to protect you. I'll come by Friday and collect the first payment." With that said the man turned and left. He stuck his head back in and added, "You sure wouldn't want that pretty assistant of yours hurt."

Lisa stared at the door after the man left. "What are you going to do, Jonathon?" Lisa was visibly upset. She had heard about gangs pulling stuff like this but she didn't think it would happen to them.

"Lisa, I heard about a gang trying to get started around here some time back and I installed some cameras. Up to now, I didn't do anything with the film, but now it's different." Jonathon took a ladder and climbed to the first camera and removed the film and instantly put in new film.

"This I'm taking to the police. On second thought, I think I'll have my friend, Sergeant Larson, come to the garage in an unmarked police car. We'll open the door for him so he can drive into one of the bays. Make sure one of them is empty."

Lisa went into the garage and found one empty bay. "Hey, fellas, don't put any car in bay two, okay."

"Whatever you say," they both answered.

Jonathon made his phone call and in a half an hour Sergeant Larson drove into the open bay in the garage and walked into the reception area.

"Okay, Jonathon, show me the film," he ordered.

Jonathon ran the film while the sergeant watched. "That's who I thought it was. He has a gang of men. I'm going to suggest each business in this area put in a camera similar to yours. This is enough to arrest the man who threatened you. If everyone has a camera inside and out we're bound to find every criminal who is involved in this extortion plot. We don't want that going on in our town!"

Jonathon agreed with him. The cameras weren't that expensive so every business should be able to afford one. He'd be pleased when all the gang of criminals were caught and behind bars. Now if all the businesses will go along with this, it should take no time at all and they would catch the crooks. This had been a good town and he hated to see it taken over by a gang of thieves.

"I'm going to stop at the businesses now and suggest they put the cameras in today. I'll give you as an example. Now, I want to come when you open on Friday and stay until the man comes to collect your donation," the sergeant suggested and smiled. "I'll arrest him on the spot and then I'll watch your garage vey carefully so that another criminal won't be able to do any harm to you. The town of Granger has been such a good place to live. All those crooks need was to get a foothold and they'll take over. Not in my town they aren't going to," the sergeant exclaimed. He sure hoped that they could stop this thing before it got started.

"I'll see you on Friday and thanks for all your help." Jonathon remarked. He watched as the Sergeant Larson left. He noticed that he stopped at the next business close to his garage. He bet that the sergeant would put a policeman in every business that the men tried to intimidate. On Friday, they would all get their come up-ins as his mother used to say.

On the way home that evening, he and Lisa stopped at several of the businesses just to see if they were all cooperating. Every one of them appeared to be so relieved that the police were doing something about this right up front. They all told him that the criminals were coming back on Friday. That ought to be an interesting day. He wondered if one man was going to pick up all the money or if several of the gang were.

The rest of the week went by smoothly. They had a little more work than they could keep up with, but Jonathon never minded that. People didn't seem to mind waiting until the next day to get there car as long as Jonathon loaned them one to use.

There didn't seem to be anything that Lisa couldn't do when it came to repairing a vehicle. She sure took to it. She was an intelligent woman and she was going to be his wife very shortly.

He knew when she was younger that she loved to vacuum the automobiles and wash the outside of them and she did a good job. But he never once thought when she grew up that she would want to be a mechanic. He sure didn't know one woman who was a mechanic but then this was a small town. There were probably several of them throughout the country.

Jonathon was anxious for Friday to come. He wanted those crooks out of his hair and into jail. He would cooperate with the police in any way he could.

When he thought about Friday he wanted to smile. He could just see the face of the criminal as he was handcuffed and led to the police car. It was going to be an interesting day.

Chapter Sixteen

The Extortionists

When Friday morning arrived there was Sergeant Larson sitting in an old beat up car as if he wanted it to be repaired. Jonathon laughed. He was going to play the scenario out to the limit. No one would think that was a police car. In fact, no one would think the old junker would even work.

Jonathon asked all the employees to step into the office for a quick meeting with the sergeant.

"I want you employees to stay in the garage when the man or men come to collect the extortion money. Don't come out. Jonathon and I will take care of this. I'm hoping to just handcuff the guy and carry him off to jail, but you never know what he might do. Please stay in the garage. I don't want anyone shot because the extortionist becomes excited and starts shooting because he doesn't want to go to jail."

Everyone agreed to do as the sergeant said. They would be curious though. "After you handcuff him, can we come out?" Lisa asked.

Leave it to Lisa, Jonathon thought. "I don't know. What do you think, sergeant?" he asked.

"It might be best if you didn't. If something goes wrong and they don't keep him in jail, he would remember you and he might come after you. Just stay in there until it's over and you hear me leave."

The crew went into the garage but Jonathon and Sergeant Larson stayed and had a cup of coffee. It was about nine o'clock when the extortionist came to collect.

"Okay, where is my money? I want to see the books to make sure you are giving me the right amount," he growled.

"I'll get the money and the books right away," Jonathon exclaimed and acted as if he was nervous. He could tell by looking at the man that he was pleased his victim was on the nervous side. Jonathon brought $300 dollars and gave to the man and let him look at the books. It wasn't his real ledger. It was a false one he had made up knowing the man would ask to see it since he had asked for a percentage instead of a specific amount. He wondered why the man would request a percentage. There must be a reason and that was probably to see how the business was doing.

As the man was busy looking at the accounting ledger, the sergeant walked over to the criminal and had handcuffed him so fast that he didn't know what hit him.

"What are you doing?" he growled at the sergeant.

"You're under arrest for forcing this man to pay you money that he doesn't owe you. That's illegal."

"He owes me this money. Now take these cuffs off of me immediately," demanded the thief.

"When you get to the police station, I'll show you the tape that we have showing you coming into his garage trying to force Mr. Livingston to take some insurance so you wouldn't burn down his garage or hurt his employees. Those threats are illegal. You just accepted $300 of extortion money. I hope they throw the book at you," the sergeant exclaimed and smiled.

The man stared at the sergeant. He had no idea that he had been filmed when he tried to force Jonathon to pay him some insurance money. He should have been more careful. He had heard about cameras being placed in some business just for that reason but in a garage? He couldn't believe it.

"I'll see you in court, Jonathon. With your testimony and that film, I'll bet we could put this guy away for fifteen to twenty years. Surely by that time he'd learn a lesson and start being honest. Once they run his finger prints, I wonder what they will find. I'll let you know." The officer winked at Jonathon and took his prisoner out and put him in the car.

"Everyone can come out now, the fun is over," Jonathon told them. "I sure hope they catch the whole bunch today. When Lisa and I stopped at several businesses on our way home that day that he had threatened us, the owners were all going to cooperate. I hope there was a different man to collect in most of the places today and that way the police would arrest them all in one day. If not, he's going to watch our garage very carefully."

The rest of the day went well. Just before they left, the sergeant called. "Jonathon, you won't believe it, but we hauled in seven of those men. Now I don't know if there are any of them left, but we have a policeman watching all of the seven businesses just in case they try to burn them down or break in. It would be nice if that was the end of it. This is terrible to say but let them go to a different town."

Jonathon laughed. If they were in a different town, they wouldn't bother the businesses here. "What type of sentence do you think they'll receive? Sergeant, if they get a short sentence they're bound to come back and try to get even with us," Jonathon remarked.

"Jonathon, I think they'll get at least ten years because they were trying to form a gang and take over the businesses. If they did as these criminals usually do, they start out with ten percent and before you know it they own your business. The judge is going to take that into consideration. I don't think you have anything to worry about. Besides that, he looked some of the men up and found they had tried this before and were wanted in some other states. Most of the men have criminal records."

That evening after work, Jonathon and Lisa stopped at a few of the places. They listened as the owners told them about the arrest. Only in one place did the police have to shoot the extortionist. But they listened to some funny tales from the other businesses in town. Each one was a little different and each criminal had a different tale to tell. My mother has nothing to eat and I was just trying to get her some food was one reason he heard. Jonathon finally went on home. He felt it had been a good day. Now what would tomorrow bring?

"That evening they talked about their wedding plans. They were to be married the next Sunday. They had everything ready. Only a few people outside of the church group were invited. Just one more week to wait, thought Lisa.

The next week went by without incident, but the police were still keeping a watch on the seven businesses just in case there were some criminals left. Sergeant Larson believed that they arrested enough of them so if there were any more they'd be discouraged and move on. This wasn't a town to fool with when it came to criminal actions.

Several of the business owners stopped by Jonathon's garage to let him know that they knew he was the one who had done a lot to stop the criminals by turning his camera film over to the police. They just wanted to thank him. They were very much relieved. Some of them had decided to pay as they didn't want to get hurt or have their businesses hurt. Then Jonathon explained that if they did pay that the extortionist would keep raising the percentage until they owned the business and the present owners would be working for them.

They were shocked to think they came that close to losing their business.

At home on Friday night, Jonathon and Lisa talked about the wedding. "Let's see, I'm supposed to say that I take this grease monkey to be my wedded wife, is that right?" Jonathon asked sincerely.

"You wouldn't dare," Lisa exclaimed and then laughed. She was quite sure he wouldn't do that or was she. "Please, Jonathon, you surely wouldn't do that to me, would you?"

Jonathon laughed. "Of course I wouldn't. I'll behave. You'll be Mrs. Jonathon Livingston, my wife. That will be so nice, Lisa. We should have done this as soon as you moved into your little apartment but I don't suppose we were ready then. You only thought of me as being your big brother and a protector. I wasn't sure how I was going to convince you that I wasn't a big brother but I was someone who was in love with you. I'm sure ready now to take on a wife."

"It's exciting isn't it? Jonathon, I always loved you but I thought you were out of my league. You were older and I was just a pest or a nuisance to you. When did I become something more than a pest?"

"When you were younger, you were a pest at times," Jonathon agreed and laughed at his fiancé. "But when I saw you on your graduation night, my heart flipped. You were so beautiful. I always loved you but that night I knew I wanted to marry you but you kept insisting that I was your big brother. I had to do something to change your mind, so I kissed you."

"That shook me up," Lisa admitted. "I thought for a while that you were just kidding around but the kiss affected me. But I figured that was the last one because you were teasing."

"But you found out different."

"Yea, I did. Now did you get any calls for you to have to work tomorrow?" Lisa asked.

"No, but Jed said he was going to bring his vehicle in Monday. I told him I wouldn't be there but I had a good crew who would take care of his vehicle."

"Where are you going to be?" Lisa asked.

"I don't know about you, but I'm going on my honeymoon," he answered with a twinkle in his eyes.

"I thought we couldn't take one now."

"I've talked to Joseph and he said he and his son could easily handle things for two days. So we'll have a two day honeymoon now and when that building is added on and we get some more mechanics, we'll take a long one. We may even take a cruise. What do you think?"

"I think that's a great plan. I'm just surprised but pleasantly so. Did you have in mind some place to go?"

"Yes, I thought we'd go to the ocean for two days. You said you loved the ocean and so do I. It doesn't take long to get there. I gave Joseph my cell phone number and if there's any problem he'll call."

Lisa went to bed that night knowing that she had only one more day before she'd be a married woman. She thought that she had the best man in the world. She wondered how she could be so fortunate.

Chapter Seventeen

The Two Orphans

Right after the Sunday morning service, the wedding took place. They had a simple ceremony but someone had decorated the church and it looked great. There were some good people in that church. The Johnson twins from the church were the flower girl and ring bearer.

Leah, Jacob's sister was Lisa's bridesmaid and Jacob was Jonathon's best man. Both of the Brown young people were so pleased to be included in the wedding. They had never done anything like that before. Leah sure loved the new dress that Lisa purchased for her. She didn't own anything like that garment.

It was a beautiful ceremony and Lisa knew she would remember it for a long time. It thrilled her when the pastor asked Jonathon if he would take Lisa Monroe as his wife and he rang out a firm I do.

After the wedding ceremony, they went into the reception room and looked at all the food and presents and the huge cake. The pastor prayed and everyone ate their dinner. Right after that they insisted the newlyweds open their presents. That took a little time. Lisa had forgotten about presents. She had only been to one or two weddings. The presents were a nice surprise.

After about two hours people began to leave. Jonathon and some of the men helped him load the presents into his car. They shook hands with the pastor and thanked him and said thanks to the rest of the group. When Jonathon started to pull out of the church parking lot, he heard a rattling noise and felt something moving underneath his car. He looked in the side mirror and noticed lots of cans and other things behind him.

Lisa was startled and cried out, "What's that noise?"

Jonathon told her about the rope tied to the car with the junk attached to it. They both got out of the car laughing. When they looked back at the church, they saw most of the people standing at the church waving and cheering. After disconnecting the rope, Jonathon drove his bride home and emptied their automobile. Now they had to put the already packed suitcases in the vehicle and they were off to the beach.

Lisa had the best time at the beach. When she took her shoes off she insisted that Jonathon take his off and they walked in the water and skipped through the waves. They had a picnic lunch on the beach and lay out in the sun in the sand and listened to the water wash up on the beach.

"This is the first time I've heard the ocean wash the sand and it sounds like music." She turned to Jonathon and stated, "I love you big boss man."

"I love you too little grease monkey," Jonathon remarked and they both laughed.

Lisa loved it all. Jonathon was so relaxed. He worked so hard at the garage that it was good for Lisa to see him relaxed and having a great time.

There were a few other sites they spent some time visiting. The two days went by fast and before they knew it they had to head back home. Perhaps they might plan to come back here for some short visits, the two agreed.

Once they arrived at the house, Lisa asked Jonathon a question. "Do you think it would be all right if I were to stay home tomorrow and get out house in order? I need to put away the presents, clean house, and do a dozen other things."

"Are you saying that I wasn't a good housekeeper?" he asked.

Lisa didn't know what to say. "You were okay. I'd just like to do a little more cleaning. When I have it like I want it, I'll be glad to be your grease monkey once again."

"You don't have to go back to the garage at all, Lisa."

"Oh, but I want to. I just may take a day off each week to catch up on the washing, ironing, housework, grocery shopping and what not. But I still want to work in the garage."

"That's fine with me. I love having my grease monkey with me wherever I am. I want you to be happy, sweetheart. I know that I'm not the best housekeeper and you need to do some deep cleaning as you ladies say. Just do whatever you want to do with the house. Move stuff around, paint the walls, do what you wish. It's your house now, darling. I had your name added to the deed. One more thing you have to do is move your things out of the apartment. What do you think? Shall we rent the apartment?"

"Why don't we wait until we find someone who really needs it unless you need the income?"

"That's a good idea. There are always people who need a place to stay. We'll do that. Sometimes the pastor asks if we know about an inexpensive apartment to rent for someone. We'll just wait a while and see if any one needs an inexpensive place to live," Jonathon agreed.

The next morning, Lisa fixed Jonathon's breakfast and kissed him goodbye. She had so many things to do that she didn't know where to start first. She really did want to paint the house but she'd do it one room at a time. First she took out the vacuum cleaner and gave the whole house a good cleaning. It did need shampooing but she didn't think Jonathon had a shampooer. Another time she would do that task. She washed windows and walls and whatever else needed washing.

Gathering all the dirty clothes she could find, she headed for the laundry room and put a load in the washer. Lisa thought how nice it was to have the whole house as hers instead of the little apartment. It was getting close to noon and she knew that she needed to get some groceries so she could fix dinner that evening. Jonathon didn't have too much in his refrigerator.

At the grocery store, she saw so many things she needed. She decided to get just a few things and return the next day. She wanted to put the roast in and have it done by the time Jonathon came home. As she drove along, she thought about her marriage and how good it was. How nice it was to be a wife and fix dinner for her husband. She had done a lot of cooking for Jonathon but never as his wife. She wished that her parents knew what a good life she had now.

It didn't take long after she returned until she had the roast in the oven along with some potatoes, carrots and onions. She made a pan of biscuits but waited to put them in until she was sure the roast was done. Oh, how she had enjoyed the day. She loved working in the garage but she loved cleaning house and being Mrs. Jonathon Livingston just as much.

Jonathon stepped in the house. "What is that good smell that I smell," he asked. He opened the oven and looked—a roast. Having a wife was a good thing he decided. From the looks on his wife's face, he came to the conclusion that she enjoyed her day cleaning house.

The dinner was enjoyable. "Did you get through with everything you wanted to do? The house looks wonderful and smells so good. The dinner is delicious. I like having a wife home cooking my dinner," he remarked and smiled.

"No, I'm going to do some more tomorrow. I'm going to take you up on that painting. Look at the living room walls. They need a good paint job," Lisa stated.

"Why don't you hire someone to help you? Painting is a hard job."

"I bet Jacob's sister Leah would help me. School is out and she probably doesn't have a lot of do. I'll do that. How did work go? I bet you didn't even miss me."

"You would lose that bet. I missed you all day. I kept wondering where my grease monkey was. It was lonesome without you," he remarked and kissed her.

"I'm glad you missed me, but what about work? Did you get everything done that you needed to?"

"Yes, we did. We didn't have as many cars as usual so we made it fine," Jonathon remarked.

The next day after Jonathon left, Lisa decided to do her grocery shopping early so she headed for the store. This time she bought everything she needed. It took a little time but she made it. Jonathon had suggested that she keep using one of the credit cards and buy the groceries with the card. That way she didn't have to worry about getting the money or worry about writing a check.

On the way home she looked down the road and it looked like an accident had just happened. A policeman was waving her to stop so she pulled to the side of the road and stepped out of the car.

"Is there anything I can do to help?" she asked.

"Yes, would you take those two children and put them in your car. Their mother was killed and I'm waiting for help from the station."

Lisa looked into the car and saw that each child had some bruises and blood on them and they were crying. She stepped into the car and unfastened the seat belts.

"You're going to go over to my car for a while," she told them and kissed each one on the cheek. She hugged them and carefully put them in her automobile. "Now tell me if you hurt any place?" she asked.

"My mommy hurts," the oldest girl said. She must be about four or five, Lisa guessed. The two year old only cried and looked at Lisa. She hugged the little one and kissed her again on the cheek and the girl smiled. Both of them liked to be hugged and kissed on the cheek. The oldest one was upset over her mother but Lisa tried to avoid saying anything about their mom. That was for the policeman to tell them about their mother. It wasn't her place to tell them their mother had died in the crash.

"Where is mommy?" she asked.

"The policeman is taking care of her. I'm going to watch you in the mean time. Now what are your names?"

"I'm Sabrina and my sister is Sissy."

"Okay, my name is Lisa." She wondered what Sissy's real name was but she wouldn't ask now. "Are you hungry?" Lisa asked.

"Yes. We didn't get any breakfast."

"I have some bread and meat. Would you like a sandwich?"

"Yes," Sabrina's eyes lit up.

Lisa quickly fixed a sandwich for Sabrina and her sister. She poured some milk in the paper cups she had purchased. The girls ate as though they hadn't eaten for a while. It made her wonder if money was tight in that home.

Finally, the police man came over to the car. "How are you doing with the girls? I see they aren't crying any more. We'll have to take them to the shelter…"

Lisa stepped out of the car.

"Don't do that, please. Do you suppose I could watch them at least for tonight? We're getting along real well and they're no longer crying. They were hungry so I fed them a sandwich. They've taken to me. It would be a shame to put them somewhere strange at this time. I think they associate me with their mother because I'm here now. Tomorrow you could decide what to do with them, but let me keep them tonight. I'm Lisa Livingston. My husband owns the garage…"

"I know your husband very well, Lisa. Okay, take the children home. They don't appear to have any broken bones so they don't need to go to the hospital. I'll try to see if they'll let me leave them with you until we can find a suitable home."

"Thank you. I'll take them home and give them a bath. They have their mother's blood on them. Give me your card in case I need to call."

She took the officer's card and drove on home. Lisa had an idea that the officer was breaking a few rules by letting her take the children but it was an easy way out for him. The ambulance had come and they were putting the mother in it. They would take her to the mortuary she assumed.

Granger was a small town. There weren't that many places where they could place orphans so the policeman was a little relieved that there was some one who took the children at least for one night. He knew the woman who usually took care of children without homes was now on a month's vacation so she couldn't help.

It amazed the officer that the children took so quickly to Lisa. He watched as she slipped back into the car. Each girl hugged her. That was good for the two little girls who didn't even know about their mother. He felt relieved that he was leaving them with someone who really cared about them.

When Lisa arrived at home, she let the oldest girl help her carry in the groceries. Sabrina seemed pleased to help. The little one wanted something to carry so Lisa gave her a small package. After several trips, everything was out of the car and into the house. Lisa hugged each of the girls and thanked them for helping her. She sat them up to the counter and dished up some ice cream.

It didn't appear that she would do any painting today. She would be babysitting. There was a double bed in one of the spare rooms.

That is where she would put the girls. She wished she had some toys for them. Would she dare take them to town and get some? Then she remembered that she had some old dolls and a few things she had kept from childhood. That would be something for them to play with right after she gave them a bath.

The two girls loved the bath. Lisa noticed that they were not all that clean. She decided to wash their clothes by hand and put them in the dryer. The girls could wrap up in towels until the clothes were dried.

"These two girls and their mother have been living on the street," Lisa decided. Every now and then she would hug the girls and they hugged her back. She took them into the room she had for them and told them to lay down for a few minutes.

"This is nice, Mrs. Lisa. We had to sleep in the car. We didn't have a bed or a house. I like your house."

That was just what she thought. "Just rest for a few minutes, okay? Your clothes will be dry in a little bit."

"It's nice to be in a bed." Sabrina was so tickled over a simple thing as a bed to sleep in.

Lisa left them and hurried into her and Jonathon's bedroom. She remembered where she put her box of sentimental toys. She took the dolls out and a ball. That would keep them entertained for today. She had some extra clothes for the dolls. The new wife could remember back when she played with the dolls, that was when she had a mother and a father. Now these two girls had neither.

As she entered their bedroom, she found the girls sound asleep. She smiled. The two probably didn't get too much sleep in a car.

Chapter Eighteen

Caring for the Girls

The phone rang and Lisa hurried to answer it. She didn't want the ring to wake up the girls.

"Hello, this is the Livingston home."

"Mrs. Livingston, this is Sergeant Larson. I wonder if you could keep the children for a day or two. The children's services have no place to put them, in fact at the present there is no service. We have searched for some relatives and we don't think there are any. Is there anyway you can take care of them for a while?" the officer asked.

"I'd be pleased to keep them. They're very good children. Officer, I think they have been living in their car. The oldest girl was so happy to have a bed. She said they usually slept in the car."

"I think you're right. There were bedding, food, change of clothes and other things that would give the appearance of them living in the car. The mother appeared to be dead. I was pretty sure but the doctor still had to check her. I'll be in touch with you. I'll bring their clothes over after a while," he promised.

The newlywed wife wondered what her husband was going to say about their visitors. It was Thursday. She had planned on going to work on Friday but not now. What would Jonathon say? He was so easy going she didn't think he would mind. It was a good thing that the two girls were so good or she'd never have agreed to take care of them.

After about two hours, she heard the girls talking in the bedroom. She stepped in quietly. They were playing patty cake with each other. She smiled.

"Mrs. Lisa," Sabrina exclaimed. "We had a nice nap. Can we get up now?"

"You sure can. I found something you can play with. Here are your clothes. Now are you hungry or do you want to wait for dinner?"

"Do we get to eat again today?" Sabrina asked.

Lisa wanted to cry. "Yes, darlings, you get to eat. You can have a snack now and then we'll have dinner after my husband gets home."

"Is he nice?" Sabrina asked as if she was frightened at the fact that a man would be coming into the house soon.

"He's a very nice man, Sabrina. You'll like him."

"Our father was mean. Then he died. But he was always hitting us and we didn't know why."

"Sabrina, I'm so sorry but Jonathon would never hit anyone," Lisa promised.

"He doesn't hit you?"

"No, darling, he doesn't. He loves me. And he'll love you too, you'll see." Lisa could see some doubt in the little face. All the men the child had to deal with were probably mean to the girl.

The two hugged the dolls. Lisa decided that she would let the girls keep them. Why she had kept them all these years she wasn't sure. Even though they were old, the girls loved them. They changed their clothes and pretended to feed them. They played with the ball very carefully rolling in across the floor.

While they were so busy, she decided she best put some dinner on the stove. She could see the children from the kitchen. She wondered why they didn't mention their mother or ask about her, especially the older one. But Sabrina said nothing about her mother since she brought her to the house. Did she know she was dead? Or was she afraid to ask?

As she prepared the food, she set the table for four. She had fixed some spaghetti, corn and a salad. She made a quick pudding for desert.

Jonathon walked into the house and headed for the living room. He saw the girls and turned and went into the kitchen. "Lisa, it takes nine months to have a baby. I see two children in our living room. They cannot possible be ours." He smiled.

"We're going to keep them for a few days."

"Okay, what's the rest of the story?"

"I was driving home from the grocery store when a policeman motioned for me to pull over at the scene of an accident. He needed help with the children." Lisa lowered her voice. "Their mother was killed in the accident. On top of that they have been living in a car. Sabrina told me that they slept in the car. Not knowing what else to do with the children, the policeman wondered if we could keep them until something was worked out. Their father is dead and they can find no relatives."

"Well, why don't we just adopt them? I always wanted a family." Jonathon made the remark as if he was serious.

"After spending the afternoon with the girls, I'd sure like to but the officer said just for a few days until they could make other arrangements. Come meet the girls. They are rather afraid of men because their father was mean to them so be real careful," Lisa advised.

Jonathon walked into the room and sat down by the girls. "Hello ladies, how are you. You have some nice looking dolls there," he stated and smiled at them.

"We're just girls, we're not ladies," Sabrina answered and smiled back at him.

"I guess you're right. Now what is your name? My name is Jonathon."

"I'm Sabrina and this is my sister. Her name is Sissy," she replied.

"What pretty names you have. Lisa tells me that you're going to spend some days with us. That should be fun. We'll have a good time. Maybe Saturday we could go to the park. What do you think?"

"That would be nice. Mrs. Lisa said you were a nice man and didn't hit people. Is that right?"

"That's right. It isn't right to hit other people, is it?"

"No," Sabrina agreed.

"Now, will your sister talk to me," asked Jonathon.

"When she knows you real well, she will. But she never talks with strangers."

That statement hit Jonathon between the eyes. He was trying not to be a stranger. How was he going to get this little gal so she would be comfortable with him? He sure loved the two little girls already. He hated the thought that they were orphans. If no one claimed them, why couldn't he and Lisa adopt them?

They sure were two pretty girls and appeared to be well behaved. They hadn't mentioned their mother and he wondered why. Did they know she was dead? That was going to be something that would be hard to tell them.

Lisa called them to come to the dinner table. Sabrina announced that they usually only had one meal a day.

Jonathon sure didn't like to hear that. A mean father and half starved children, it wasn't fair. "Well, now you get to eat three times a day."

"Really?" Sabrina asked.

"Really." They washed up and headed for the table. The two bowed their heads as Jonathon prayed over the meals. The girls ate very nicely but said nothing during the whole dinner time.

Jonathon tried to start a conversation.

"We aren't supposed to talk at the table," Sabrina informed him.

"At this table, Sabrina, you may talk. We always talk at our table and you can too. We don't have a lot of rules."

Sabrina looked at him and smiled. "That's nice."

When they finished their meal they went into the living room. Jonathon turned the television on. The girls stared at it as if they had never seen a TV before. Once the news was over, he looked for a children's program and found a cartoon. They looked up at him and smiled and watched the cartoon for about an hour. Jonathon looked down and saw two very sleepy children so he turned the television off.

"I think it is bedtime," he stated.

Lisa and Jonathon both went into the bedroom with the girls. "We're going to pray before you go to sleep," Jonathon told them. He sat on the bed and said a little pray that included the girls. When he was through, he said amen. Lisa opened the covers and let the girls slip into the bed and kissed them goodnight.

Sissy said, "Goodnight." That was the first word that either of them heard her say. She must be feeling just a little more comfortable with them.

Sabrina informed them that Sissy really liked them or she wouldn't have said goodnight to them.

Lisa and Jonathon walked back into the living room. "Well, what do you think of your new family," Lisa asked.

"Lisa, if no one wants those children and no one has a claim on them, I think we should adopt them."

"Really, I'd love to. It doesn't take long to love them, does it? Even more so when you think of the way they have had to live—sleeping in the car, one meal a day, a father who hit them. You sure you wouldn't mind a ready made family?" Lisa asked watching her husband's reaction.

"No, but my little grease monkey, that would mean you would become a mother instead of a grease monkey."

"It's a tough choice but I think I'll choose to be a mother'" Lisa answered smiling.

"We need to talk to the judge the first thing in the morning before they make some other plans to put the children in a temporary home. Have they asked about their mother, sweetheart?"

"Only at the scene of the accident, Sabrina said her mother was hurting when I asked if she was hurt. But since then they haven't mentioned their mother. I think that's strange. I don't know whether we should bring the subject up or wait a while. Perhaps in a few days they may ask. What do you think?"

"Let's wait a while. There may be a reason why they aren't asking. They might be afraid they'd have to go back and sleep in the car. We'll wait another day or so and if we feel it's right, we'll talk to them about her." Jonathon suggested.

Chapter Nineteen

The Adoption

The next morning, Jonathon went to see Judge Watson. The judge greeted him cordially. He had known Jonathon since he was a child.

"What can I do for you, my friend," the judge asked.

"Judge, we have two girls named Sabrina and Sissy that we're taking care of because of an automobile accident that killed their mother. We were told that they have no relatives. Lisa and I would like to adopt them. What are our chances?" Jonathon asked.

"I see no reason why you can't adopt them. Bring them in Monday and I'll have the paperwork for you to sign and we'll make it legal. The children's director who usually takes care of orphan children is on vacation. I wondered what we'd do with the children while she was gone, but I know of no people more qualified than you and Lisa. I'll see you Monday morning, Jonathon."

Jonathon left and immediately called Lisa and told her the good news. She was thrilled. The new mother knew that the children had nothing decent to wear. She would need to take the children to the department store and purchase each of them some new clothes. She wanted them to look perfect in front of the judge.

They also wanted to take them to church and the girls certainly didn't have anything decent to wear. So after Jonathon hung up she took the girls shopping. The two couldn't imagine having some new clothes. They laughed and giggled as they tried on different outfits.

When Jonathon came home, they had to show him all the new clothes that they had. He patiently let them show him every piece and then announced how pretty it was and how beautiful they would look in the new outfits.

Going to church was a new experience for the two girls and they weren't sure what they were supposed to do. Lisa took them to the children area and stayed for a while to give the two girls time to get acquainted. Soon they were playing with the other children and had made some friends. She hoped when it was time to sit down and listen to the teacher tell the Bible story they would both do so without argument.

When they returned home, Lisa asked the girls how they liked church time. "Did you have a good time and learn a Bible story?" she asked.

"It was real nice and the teachers were nice. Can we go back again?" Sabrina asked.

"We go every Sunday and you can go with us," Lisa promised.

The girls walked over and hugged Lisa and Jonathon. He began to enjoy the hugs from those two girls.

The next morning Jonathon drove his family to the courthouse and brought them before Judge Watson. He looked at the pretty girls. He was quite sure they weren't dressed like when they had the accident. Lisa must have purchased them some new clothes. According to the policeman from the accident, the girls were all but dressed in rags. They needed a bath and they looked as though they hadn't eaten regularly.

"I want to interview the girls first," the judge stated.

"What does inview mean?" Sabrina asked.

"The judge wants to ask you some questions. You just answer him, okay?" Jonathon instructed her.

The little girl looked up at the judge just a little frightened.

"Sabrina, how do you like your new home with Jonathon and Lisa?"

The girl's eyes lit up. "It's so nice and they love us. Mr. Jonathon doesn't hit us like our father did before he died. Mrs. Lisa doesn't take dope and she feeds us three times a day instead of once. We would like to stay with them always. Can we stay with them or do we have to go somewhere else?"

The judge wiped a tear from his eyes. What those poor little girls went through no one really knew. Now they would have a home and it would be a good one. "Do you know what it means to have someone adopt you?" he asked.

"Yes, that would mean we have a new mamma and daddy."

"That's right, Sabrina, so if it's all right with you Jonathon and Lisa are going to adopt you."

"It's all right with us, isn't it, Sissy?"

Sissy nodded her head. She didn't understand what was going on but she'd agree with her sister.

"Judge, did you find out what Sissy's real name is?"

"It's Sissy. Their last name is Brothers," the judge replied.

The adoption papers were signed. "Now there is a six month period when some relative could come and claim them. It's my duty to tell you that. But I have had my staff search the internet for relatives and have found none. It appeared that both the mother and father each were the only child of their individual parents. We found that both of their parents have long passed away. So I don't think you have to worry about some relative coming for them."

Jonathon thanked the judge and drove his new family home. He was so pleased. He held Sabrina's hand as he walked her into the house.

The girl looked up at him. "Now can we call you daddy?" she asked.

"You sure can, sweetheart," Jonathon answered and hugged the little girl. He soon headed back to the garage. It was nice to have Joseph and Jacob both working at the garage. It allowed him to get away and attend to other business without closing down his shop.

For the next two weeks all went well. The girls were happy and they fit right in the family. It seemed to Lisa that they had been there for longer than two weeks. Sabrina wanted to help clean the house and do dishes. Lisa let her while Sissy watched what she was doing. Sissy usually stayed right by Sabrina but now she was beginning to wander over to Lisa now and then.

"Mamma," Sissy said.

"Yes, Sissy, what did you want?"

"You're our mamma."

"Yes, darling, I am." It was nice to hear Sissy talk a little more. She knew the girl could talk because she could hear the two talking in the living room.

There was a knock on the door and Lisa walked to the door and opened it. There stood a woman she had never met before. The woman didn't look any too friendly. It was almost as if she had come for a fight.

"I've come for the children," she stated firmly.

Lisa wasn't quite sure what the woman meant. How could she come for the children that she and Jonathon adopted? Who was this woman anyway? She wasn't about to give the two children to some stranger who asked for them.

Chapter Twenty

Virginia Mason

"We've adopted Sabrina and Lisa Brothers and they are ours now," Lisa stated with a tone of authority. She had no idea who that woman was and she wasn't about to give the two children to her or anyone else.

"The adoption is all wrong. I'm Virginia Mason and I just returned home from a long vacation. The judge had no business letting you adopt those girls. They have to go through my department before they can be adopted so therefore the adoption is null and void. Now get the children and their things and I'll take them to the children's home," Virginia ordered.

When she found that Jonathon and Lisa had adopted two girls, she was infuriated. How could the judge make some decision without her authority? She was the only one in Granger that handled adoption. The judge ought to know that.

"The children will stay with me because I'm now their mother and Jonathon is their father. Now if you wish, I'll drive them to Judge Watson's court and we'll let him decide this. There is no way I'm going to hand my children over to you without a court order." Lisa looked at the woman but she didn't smile.

"Very well, if that's what it takes we shall go see the judge. I'll meet you there," Mrs. Mason suggested.

Lisa drove to the judge's chamber. She couldn't understand this lady. Why would she care that the children were taken care of when she was on vacation? Why did it upset her so much? It didn't make any sense to her but there was no way she would turn the children over to this woman without orders from the judge. And it would break her heart if the judge ordered her to do so.

Once they were in the Judge Watson's courtroom, Virginia Mason started in on the judge. "How could you adopt children out without my permission," she asked him angrily.

"If I remember right, you were on vacation and the children needed a home right away. Jonathon and Lisa Livingston requested that they be able to adopt the two girls and since I knew them and knew they would be excellent parents, I allowed them to adopt the girls." The judge didn't quite understand why Mrs. Mason was so upset. She had always been rather friendly before.

"You had no right to do that. Now I want you to cancel that adoption and turn the girls over to me. I have a list of people waiting to adopt children and they should have first chance. Now undo the mistake that you made," she ordered.

"Mrs. Mason, I will not change the adoption. Jonathon and Lisa are great parents and the children have bonded with them. The adoption will stand. You have no authority except what I give you."

"You had no right to do that judge. That isn't the way things work in the adoption program. Any adoption has to go through my office. You should know that by now. I thought you understood that."

"Mrs. Mason, your whole office amounts to one person—you. You alone take care of the children. Now I'm asking you to please leave now without any more objections to the adoptions that I made and leave the Livingstons alone. That's a court order."

"I'll not leave until you undo those two adoptions. It was such a stupid idea. I can't see how you can be a judge and not realize there are certain steps to take when there's an adoption."

"Mrs. Mason, you're in contempt of court. Sam, I want you to handcuff Mrs. Mason and lock her up in jail for two days. That will give her some time to think about who is in charge in this court room." The judge watched as Sam came over and handcuffed the woman.

"You can't do that to me. Stop that," she yelled but no one paid any attention to her. The officer led her off to jail.

"Lisa, you may take the children home now. I'll see that she doesn't bother you again." Lisa took her two girls and left. She was pleased that that was settled.

The judge turned and looked at the policeman that always stayed close by the courtroom. "Michael, I want you to do me a favor. I'll give you a search warrant and you go to Mrs. Mason's home and look through her files. Find out the name of all the people who adopted children from her. When people get as irate as this woman, there must be money involved. I should have looked into this before but it never dawned on me she was doing anything wrong. Check on all the people that have adopted children and see if they paid more than the $500 the county charges for adoption of children."

Michael took the warrant and headed for the Mason home. He had several keys that could unlock about any door. He found the right one and went into the office. He looked through the files and found twenty different adoptions. All of them had $500 written on the paper. He looked for other papers but found none.

The man wrote down every address and headed toward the first home. When he knocked at the door, a lady came and opened it.

"Good morning, Mrs. James, I'm just checking on adopted children. Now you went through Mrs. Virginia Mason, right?"

"Yes, is there something wrong?"

"Oh, no, I just have to follow up on this. Now what was the fee you paid? We have things written down, but this is a new rule. You know how that goes," Michael said nonchalantly.

"Oh, we paid the usual $5,000. That's what she said it always costs."

"Now the child you adopted is doing all right in your home?" Michael asked.

"Oh, yes, he's a good boy and we enjoy him so much. We couldn't have children and he was an answer to our prayer."

"Very good," the court officer remarked. "Thanks for answering my questions." He turned and left the home.

The next name on his list was Stephen and Esther Miller. Mrs. Miller was home and came to the door with a pretty girl who was all eyes looking at the visitor.

"Mrs. Miller, I'm checking on children that have been adopted out. It's a follow up. Has everything been working out with the child," Michael asked.

"Oh, my yes it sure has. Just look at this beautiful girl. She was only a baby when we were able to adopt her. We love her very much. Her name is Marie."

"Now let's see, how much did the adoption cost?"

"Oh, the usual $5,000 that everyone has to pay to adopt a child. That's what Mrs. Mason said all the adoption costs. We were glad to pay that much money for this beautiful daughter of ours."

"She is a beautiful girl indeed. Now if I can get you to sign this paper I can be on my way. I have a few other follow ups to do. I'm pleased that the adoption worked out so well for you." Michael waited for the signature and then left the Miller home.

He was able to go to ten of the homes that day. Every person who adopted a child had paid $5,000 instead of the $500 that was required. He could hardly wait to see the judge.

Chapter Twenty-One

Searching for Evidence

Once Michael returned to the courtroom that day, the judge was waiting for him. There was no real reason for Mrs. Mason to get so upset because two children were adopted out while she was on vacation unless there was money involved.

As soon as Michael stepped through the door, the judge asked, "Tell me, Michael, was my suspicions right? Was Mrs. Mason taking in more money than she was supposed to?"

"You were absolutely right, Judge Watson. She charged all ten of the people I questioned today the sum of $5,000. She turned only $500 into the county funds. The papers at her house had only $500 written on them. I had people sign the paper you gave me on the amount and how the child was doing. No one objected and no one thought $5,000 was too much money. They were pleased to have a child."

"What do you suppose Mrs. Virginia Mason will tell us? She's going to be one shocked lady. I imagine she thought no one would ever have learned about her scheme to get more money than she was entitled to."

"I can hardly wait to find out. You gave her two days, do you want me to hurry through the rest of the people who adopted children or are you going to charge her for these crimes first."

"I'm going to have her come to the court tomorrow and charge her on 20 counts of extortion. We'll see what she has to say. The thing is, if she hadn't thrown such a fit over those two girls that I adopted to the Livingstons, we'd never even looked into her adoptions policies. But I imagine she could see $10,000 just flying out the window and she couldn't live with that," the judge stated.

The next morning, Virginia Mason faced the judge. She was still mad because he placed her in prison for two days. She had every intention of giving him a piece of her mind for jailing her. Contempt of court, she'd show him how contemptible his court was. She had a plan.

"I think you owe me an apology for putting me in prison when I was only trying to follow the law," Mrs. Mason declared the minute she faced the judge.

"Was charging the parents who adopted the children $5,000 instead of $500 following the law?" the judge asked.

Virginia paled. She couldn't say anything. If they found out that was true, she could hardly deny it. The judge casually handed her copies of the papers that the parents had signed. She backed up and sat down. Then she stood back up. "I want a lawyer. He'll explain everything." She said no more.

"You are remanded to prison until this is sorted out. You may call your lawyer or if you can't afford one, one will be appointed to you but with the amount of money you received from each child you adopted out, I would think you could well afford a lawyer. I'd suggest that you get a good one."

Michael led Mrs. Mason back to prison. She wished she hadn't made such a fuss over everything now. They'd have never known if she had let the adoption of those two girls alone but she couldn't. She didn't want the judge adopting any more children without her say so. She figured if she told him outright that he couldn't adopt anyone without her permission, he would go along with her. Now she had an idea she'd be in prison for a long time. Twenty counts of extortion would cost her at least twenty years and quite possibly a lot more than that.

The judge made a call to Jonathon's garage. He told him everything that happened and that Mrs. Mason would be in prison for quite some time no matter how good of a lawyer she had. "She won't be bothering you again, Jonathon."

"Thanks, Judge Watson. My wife didn't think there would be a problem but she was a little upset when the lady came to the house demanding that Lisa give her the two girls. That shook her up some but she was pretty sure the adoption was legal and would be final in six months. Thanks again." Jonathon hung up the phone and then called Lisa and let her know the news.

"Jonathon, the girls are having such a good time. I bought them a few toys and some color books and crayons along with a blackboard. Sabrina is going to be going to kindergarten this fall and I wanted to start teaching her some of her letters. They keep asking when their daddy is coming home. Doesn't that sound good?"

"It sure does to me," Jonathon remarked. He hadn't realized you could love a couple of kids that weren't even yours as much as he loved those two girls.

When he returned home that evening, the girls were there to give him a hug and a kiss on the cheek. He loved being a father. But he did hope that one day Lisa and he would have another child. He sure wouldn't mind having a son along with the two girls. But he would wait for a while. Lisa had to get used to being a mother.

The girls went back to playing while Jonathon went into the kitchen to talk with Lisa. "I didn't tell you everything that the judge said. Did you know that Mrs. Mason was charging the people who adopted children from her $5,000 instead of $500? Boy, I think she'll be in prison for a long time. Michael talked to ten different people today. Her records showed that she had adopted twenty children to different people and each one gave her $500. But the adoptive parents all said they paid $5,000. No wonder she was so mad that the judge adopted the girls to us. She didn't get her $10,000 that she would have if the adoption had gone through her."

"She'll be fortunate if she only serves twenty years. I'm pleased that I don't have to deal with her anymore. Virginia Mason thought she could come right in my house and take the girls just like that and I was supposed to let her do it. Not my children, no way was she going to get them."

The judge called and asked that Lisa attend the hearing that would be held for Virginia Mason. He'd have one of the ladies who worked at the courthouse watch the girls while she attended the Mason trial. He didn't think he needed her to testify but he couldn't be sure. Mrs. Mason had retained one of the lawyers that didn't always put the whole truth across and the judge felt that he needed some back up. He had Michael pick three of the parents that he thought would be best for testifying against the woman. When they found out how much she had over charged them, they were only too wiling to agree to be in court and testify.

It was one month later that the court trial would take place. They were rushing this through as it seemed to be an open and shut case but the judge knew that Lawyer Dick Knowlton wouldn't let it be too open and shut. He would counter everything that was said.

Lisa sat in the crowd waiting for the trial to begin. In only a few minutes, Jonathon joined her. "Everything is going great at the garage so I thought I'd sit in for a few minutes and see how things are going here in court. Do you think Mrs. Virginia Mason looks just a trifle nervous?"

"The woman knows she was caught red handed," Lisa answered. "I can't imagine what kind of defense she's going to have. But she's a fast talker. There's no telling what kind of tale she'll come up with."

District Attorney Ronald Ashton was the first one to speak. He simply told a few facts and then asked the three parents how much money they were charged. Lawyer Knowlton questioned each one thoroughly.

"Are you quite sure you paid Mrs. Mason $5,000. Where is your proof? Do you have a check or money order receipt?"

"Yes, I have a bank receipt for my payment," answered the first parent.

"Are you sure that was for the adoption. Couldn't you have owed Mrs. Mason for something else?"

"I never met Mrs. Mason before or after the adoption. I just heard that there was a child that needed adopting and we went to her office. Right on the receipt it says for adoption of Stacy Long. I don't know what other proof you want. I didn't make the check up. You can see where it cleared through the bank. Please tell me what other proof you want me to show you."

All three of the witnesses were given the same drill trying to make it look as though everyone was out to get Mrs. Mason and that she didn't really charge anyone any more than $500 for the adoption.

The District Attorney looked at the jury. They weren't buying the defense's story at all. They were frowning at the defense attorney as he tried to bow beat the parents as he questioned them.

Then the defense attorney did something shocking. "I want to call Judge Watson to the stand. Could you get someone to fill in while you're being queried?"

"Dick, what possible reason do you want me to testify? I knew nothing of the conditions of the adoptions. That was Mrs. Mason's doings. I never checked on her because she appeared to be doing a good job with the children and with the adoption. How do you think I can help her?"

"Judge, according to Mrs. Mason, you overstepped your bounds when you adopted two children out without going through her office. You should have put the children in a temporary home until she returned from vacation. You were at fault," Dick answered.

The judge smiled. "Would you like to look at the requirements of my position as judge, Dick? It includes adopting children to prospective parents. I don't have to go through any agency at all. Do you want me to read it to you?"

"I suppose not. If you had the authority, we can't challenge you. In Mrs. Mason's defense, I'd like to announce how little she was getting paid for doing her job. She barely received enough to feed and clothe the children while she was taking care of them before adopting them out. I feel this whole thing is very unfair to her and she is being railroaded. Twenty counts of extortion and you only had three of them testify." Dick knew he was grasping at straws but any doubt he could place in the jury's mind was worth a try.

"I'll call the other seventeen if you wish, Dick, and you can query them but I'm telling you, they'll have the same story as these three. And Mrs. Mason made $49,000 a year which is a good salary in this small town of Granger."

"Forty-nine thousand dollars," Dick Knowlton repeated and looked at Virginia. Evidently she had given him a different number. "That won't be necessary. The defense rests." The woman lied to him. How could he defend her when she lied? He had no doubt that she was guilty now but he was required to give her the best defense he could and he did.

In one hour the jury was back and Mrs. Virginia Mason was declared guilty on all twenty accounts of extortion. The judge thanked the jury and Sam led the angry woman back to her cell. She was sure that Dick Knowlton had enough tricks up his sleeve to get her out of this but evidently not.

This wasn't over as far as she was concerned. She would call for an appeal and get a better lawyer. Perhaps she could plead insanity because of all the problems she had while taking care of the children before they were adopted out.

Yes, that was what she would do. She would have the next lawyer say that she was under so much stress that she didn't know what she was doing.

"Mr. Knowlton, I want you to put in an appeal for me," Mrs. Mason requested of her defense lawyer.

"Virginia, you'll have to get a different lawyer. You lied to me. If you were making as little wages as you claimed you might have had a chance of getting the charge lowered but your lie is why the jury found you guilty. I'm not sure you can find any lawyer who will work on an appeal unless he does it just to get your money. He'll never win the case."

Mrs. Mason just stared at the man. There had to be a way that she could get out of serving all that time. She couldn't stand the idea of going to prison. Just one night in jail was enough. What if she promised to pay back the money? That was something to think about.

Chapter Twenty-Two

A Big Surprise

Lisa was having a good time being the mother of the two girls. Sometimes she took them to the garage to see how things were going. She'd love to go work on a vehicle but she'd rather be a mother. Both the girls loved to come to the shop where their daddy worked.

They watched him carefully and were allowed to go into the garage to see what he was doing. They weren't satisfied just to be in the reception area. Lisa tried her best not to interfere with the working mechanics but she just had to visit the garage from time to time. That was her lifesaver when she was twelve because Jonathon would give her twenty dollars. He never knew how many groceries she could buy with that money and how badly the money was needed at that time.

Then when both her parents were gone, there was the mechanic job. And there was where she and Jonathon grew close. Yes, it was a good place to come and visit. Jonathon never seemed to mind her stopping by with the girls. Sabrina and Sissy were always begging to go to the garage and watch daddy work on cars. Lisa couldn't quite figure out why they were fascinated by the garage and the workers but they were and she wouldn't discourage them.

A year had passed since they adopted the two girls. Sabrina was now in the first grade and always came home with lots of things to tell her parents. Through the whole year there was never a mention of their birth mother. It was as if they had forgotten about her. The only thing that Lisa could think of as to why they never mentioned her was because they had such a good life now instead of living in a car with a mother who took dope. Perhaps they were afraid they would have to go back to that life if they said too much about their mother.

Another year went by. It seemed that the girls had always been with them. Lisa took enough trips to the garage to keep in touch. Once in a while she would work on an automobile and let Jonathon watch the girls. When Sissy went to school next year she would spend some time in the garage, she decided. Just once in a while it made her feel better to work on a vehicle. It was nonsense she knew, but she loved doing it.

Lisa woke up one morning not feeling too good and decided just to feed every one cold cereal. She didn't remember being with anyone who had the flu but that was just what she felt she had.

"Darling, do I need to stay home with you," Jonathon asked.

"No, I'll be fine. I'll take some cold medicine or a couple of aspirins and I'll be okay. You drop Sabrina off at the school at nine and I'm sure Sissy and I will have a nice quiet day. I'll rest on the couch."

After Jonathon left, Sissy came over and patted her mother's hand. "Mamma sick? I take care of you. I bring you water."

Oh, dear, how will she get some water and will she used a clean cup to put it in, Lisa wondered. She watched as the girl picked up the step ladder and climbed up it enough to reach the faucet and the cupboard. She retrieved a clean glass and then turned on the faucet and filled it up about three fourths full. Then she proudly backed down the steps and brought the water to Lisa.

"That's very good, Sissy. Thank you. That does taste good. Now Mamma is going to rest until time to make us some sandwiches. That's still three hours away. Can you play right here close to me?"

"I make the samwiches," Sissy declared.

"Darling, we'll do it together when it's lunchtime."

Lisa could just picture what that sandwich might look like if Sissy made it by herself although she did a good job getting the water. At least the water seemed to settle her stomach and she was feeling pretty good. She stood up. She had expected to feel poorly the whole day. That was a short flu spell to say the least.

Sissy was putting a puzzle together and then tearing it up and starting over. Then she wrote on the black board. She was writing the letters that Lisa taught to Sabrina. That was interesting. She wondered if she knew the names of the letters.

"Sissy, what is that letter that you just wrote?"

"That's N and that's A and that's a B."

"How did you know that?" Lisa asked.

"Sabrina showed me. She had me write on the board and say what each letter was. She wants me to know what she knows. She teaches me every day what she learns in school."

"That's great, darling. You keep learning." So that was why they spent so much time in the family room with the chalk board. Lisa was amazed. By the time Sissy went to school, she would know everything Sabrina knew.

She was pleased that the two argued very little. Sissy seemed to feel that Sabrina was her old sister so she should do what she said. However, a time or too she didn't want to and then they had a quarrel. Lisa usually tried to let them settle it.

After Lisa cleaned house she told Sissy it was time they made the sandwiches. "Sissy, you have to wash your hands before you make the sandwiches. Now let's both of us wash our hands.

When the hands were clean, she let the girl spread the mayonnaise on the bread. Lisa was surprised at what a good job she did. Then she let her put the meat and cheese on the sandwiches along with some lettuce. She looked at what Sissy did and decided that she couldn't have done any better. The tot didn't even make a mess on the table. She couldn't believe it.

When the sandwiches were finished, Sissy announced, "I will pray over the samwiches."

Lisa was shocked but tried not to show it.

"All right, you pray over our food," Lisa agreed. This was a first but then there were many firsts when it came to Sissy. She was always surprised with what that girl came up with.

"Bless the food and bless mamma and bless me. Amen." Sissy looked up at her mother for approval.

"Sissy, that was a good prayer. Now let's eat." That girl never stopped amazing Lisa. She was a lot smarter than she had given her credit for. Sissy had been so quiet that Lisa was afraid that she was a little slow but now that she was talking she could tell there was nothing slow about the girl. Perhaps she would train her in a few house work duties if she appeared to want to do them.

She needed to do some wash so after lunch she let Sissy help her sort the clothes and then put the clothes in the washer. She poured the soap in a cup and let Sissy put the soap in the washing machine and then Lisa started the washer.

"I wash the clothes," Sissy announced.

"You sure did, darling. And after they are washed, we shall put them in the dryer and then when they are dry we'll fold them and put them away or hang them up. You can help me fold them."

"Oh, good, I'm a good helper, huh?" Sissy asked.

"You're a great helper, sweetheart."

When Jonathon and Sabrina walked through the door, Sissy was right there to meet them. Jonathon hugged Sissy and then he had to hug Sabrina as well and then hugged their mother.

"How are you feeling, dear?" Jonathon asked.

"I'm fine now. I don't know what the matter was with me this morning but I'm fine now. I want Sissy to tell you what she did today," Lisa suggested.

"I took care of mamma because she was sick. I brought mamma a glass of water. I helped her make samwiches. And I did the wash and fold clothes." Sissy was so proud of her accomplishments.

"Is that right? Wow, our little girl is growing up. I'm proud of you, Sissy," Jonathon said and hugged the girl.

The next morning, Lisa didn't feel good once again. Now this is silly, she thought. She knew she didn't have a fever. How come she felt bad in the morning? She slept just fine last night. Well, she wasn't going to mention it to anyone. It would sound like she was looking for sympathy. She always hated it when someone was sick and demanded attention.

Sabrina helped her put the eggs, bacon and toast on the table. The girl had even set the plates on the table for her properly placing the silverware around the plates. Sabrina loved doing that. They all sat down and Sissy said she would pray. Jonathon looked at her and nodded his head.

"Bless the food. Bless Sabrina. Bless mamma. Bless daddy. Bless me. Amen," she said and looked at her dad.

"That was a good prayer, Sissy. Mamma, I think she said everything that needed to be said in that prayer."

"She sure did."

Sabrina hugged her sister. She was so pleased that now her sister would talk to people. But sometimes she talked a little too much. Sabrina could remember when she would say nothing to anyone but her and she had to tell the people what Sissy wanted or needed.

The next morning it was the same sick feeling but Lisa decided she wasn't going to let it get her down. Since she always felt better during the day time, she wasn't going to worry about feeling a little under the weather in the mornings. She drove Sabrina to school and told her that she would come and pick her up in the evening. There was no need for Jonathon to have to do that every day because she had problems with her mornings.

The next morning, she really felt bad. She ate her breakfast and before she finished, Lisa ran to the bathroom. There in the commode was her breakfast—every bit of it.

"What do you think, dear, seven or eight months more?" Jonathon laughed and looked at his peeked wife.

Lisa had begun to suspect that she might be pregnant but she wasn't positive. "You just think you're so smart, don't you?" They both laughed.

"Now let's talk about this. I really do need a boy but these girls are so good I suppose I could put up with another one. But how about trying for a boy? Do you think you could do that?" He smiled at Lisa and watched her. He had thought that she didn't feel good the last few days but she said nothing so he went on to work. She had been a little paler than usual.

"You'll get whatever the good Lord gives us, Mr. Big Boss Man," she stated firmly with her hands on her hips.

"Yeah, my little grease monkey, but I can pray for a boy. Now Lisa, make an appointment and see the doctor. He can give you something for your upset stomach and make sure you have the right vitamins. When you go, bring the girls to the garage and I'll watch them. They love the garage as you know. They are very good and they know where they can go and what they can touch. My girls are very obedient," he announced. "I sure hope my boy will be too."

"Actually, three girls don't sound too bad. That way I can pass the clothes from Sissy down to Aubrey and we wouldn't have to buy any for a girl but I don't suppose you're going to let me dress your boy in Sissy's clothes."

"You have a name for the girl all ready? That means I have to pick out a name for the boy. Let's see. How about Justin Jonathon Livingston? Now there's a name," Jonathon remarked smiling.

"Justin. I always liked that name. Okay if it's a boy, we'll name him Justin. I rather like his middle name too," Lisa declared.

"What do you mean if...?"

Chapter Twenty-Three

Working at Home

Lisa received a call the next morning from the judge. She was surprised to hear his voice. "Mrs. Livingston, I'd like you to come see me but first I want to see if you're willing to take a position that desperately needs to be filled."

"You can call me, Lisa, judge. Now what position is this?"

"It's Virginia Mason's position. There aren't a lot of children that become orphans in our small town but from time to time we do have them. There's been a woman who has taken care of two children during the last two years and I've signed adoption papers for them but the woman is ill and no longer able to take care of the children even for a day or two."

"That's too bad. I think I'd be interested," Lisa replied.

"We need some woman to take care of them until we find a qualified couple who wants to adopt a child. Now I have a list of people that came from Mrs. Mason's files. That would be a good place to start."

The judge must know a little more than I thought he did. He's already planning on me taking the job. "I'll be there soon, judge. Is it all right to bring my two children with me?"

"You may bring them. Let's set the time at eleven if that is okay with you," the judge suggested.

"I'll be there at eleven."

Lisa hurried and made sure the children were dressed appropriately and put them in her automobile. She wanted to stop by the garage and talk with Jonathon. She wondered what he would say about her taking on this position.

Jonathon saw her drive up and went to walk the kids into the garage.

"We're not here for a visit. I just need to talk with you. The judge called me and he wants…"

Jonathon interrupted, "Is something wrong?" he asked.

"Oh, no, he wondered if I could take over Virginia Mason's job but only the part of the job that includes caring for the children and finding people to adopt them. Her other jobs have been covered by other workers. I'm going now to have a talk with him. He said it was fine to bring the girls."

Sabrina spoke up. "We want to stay with daddy."

"We don't have too much work. Let them stay here. Now I want to warn you about one part of the job that you haven't considered. You can't get attached to these children. If you do, you'll be crying every time someone comes to get them. Now I'd advise you to interview several of the people on Mason's list and have someone ready to take them. I know you, darling, you won't want to give the children up once you care for them for a day or two."

"Believe it or not, I think you're right. I did think about it and I'm going to make myself understand that I can't take every orphan in the county."

"Good."

Lisa left the girls as they requested and went on to the judge's chamber. It was a holiday and she was surprised that he was working but knowing Judge Watson, he was always busy. He never kept certain hours but worked long after he should be home. Since he was a widower he spent more hours at work than at home.

As she walked into the judge's court room, he welcomed her. "Where are the girls," he asked.

"I stopped at the garage to talk with Jonathon first and they wanted to stay with their father. The girls love him. He always gives them a job to do or something to keep them occupied when they go to the garage."

"Well, I was hoping to get to see them. I guess I'll have to go to the garage if I want to see how they've grown. Now, Lisa, you may go a year or two and not have any children. You don't have to go to an office or anything. We'll call you when there is a child. I have a rule book that I need you to learn and follow. I thought we'd pay you by the hour from the time I call you about the children until they leave for their adopting parents. Would that be sufficient?"

"That's just fine, judge. My husband has warned me not to get to attached to the children and find someone ahead of time that's waiting for a child. I think that's probably what I should do. I love children."

"Would you believe that Mrs. Mason wasn't all that fond of children? She always hired someone to take care of them if they were to be in her home more than a day or two. I just found that out not too long ago. Now here is the packet that you need to read and study. There aren't a lot of rules but there are some. They mostly pertain to the prospective parents and if they're the proper people and have a good home and a good income to support the children. You need to make sure they're not heavy drinkers. That takes a little investigating."

"That sounds interesting. I promise to read it thoroughly. You call me when you have a child and I'll come pick the child up," Lisa promised.

"Someone will probably bring the boy or girl to you. That's the way it worked in the past. So do as your husband said and interview someone so you'll have a prospective parent for the child ahead of time. Be sure and keep tract of the time you spend locating a parent and the gas mileage as well," the judge instructed.

"Oh, I don't need to be reimbursed for all…"

"Yes you do. That's part of the job and I want it documented. That's how we keep these positions and how we get money to fund this position. You're to keep track of all expenses incurred in the adoption, understood?"

"Yes, sir, I do." Lisa didn't quite know what to say. It seemed petty to put all that down but she could understand funding the position and having enough hours to qualify. She would do as she was told even if it was a little petty.

After leaving the courthouse she drove to the garage. There were her girls sweeping the reception room and picking up papers. They thought they were big people to be able to work in a garage. There was no doubt but that the two took after her when it came to enjoying being at the garage. They appeared to love every minute of the time they spent there.

"You just wanted the girls so you could work them," Lisa accused her husband. "You know there is a child labor law. They have to be so old before you can make them work."

"Those girls will never tell on me. Free labor is always good. I had some free labor out of you until you got to washing cars and vacuuming them. I'm good at getting things done for free," he remarked and hugged her.

"Can we stay longer, mamma?"

"Now see what you've done. They don't want to go home," Lisa remarked and laughed.

"It's lunch time. Why don't you go across the street and buy us all a sub and a drink and we'll have lunch together." What do you say?" Jonathon asked.

"You do come up with some good ideas."

Lisa walked across the street and picked up the subs and the drinks and added a few cookies. Sometimes Jonathon took his lunch but often he would grab a sub. She would have thought that he would get tired of eating them but he never did. She had to admit they were good sandwiches and pretty healthy as well.

The two girls thought it was the neatest thing to be able to eat at the garage. They had never done that before. They sat on the bench and ate and watched everything that was going on in the reception room.

A customer came in and looked at the girls. "Jonathon, don't you think they're a little young to be working in your garage?" Mike asked.

"I never turn down free labor, Mike."

Mike laughed and talked with the girls for a while. He was impressed with them. He walked over to Jonathon. "Do they quarrel with each other?"

"Not much but once in a while they do. I imagine as they get older they might argue more but they're pretty good kids right now. But, Mike, we aren't fooling ourselves. We know there'll be some problems from time to time. Everyone talks about the teen years. I'm hoping to keep them in church and hopefully they will be Christians and want to get along with each other and their parents. I can only hope and pray that will happen."

Mike told him what was wrong with his automobile and Jonathon gave him a form to fill out and Mike gave him the car keys.

"That food smells so good, I'm going across the street and get me a sub," he told the girls and left the garage.

"You can come back and eat with us," Sabrina told him.

"I wish I had the time but I have an appointment and have to leave. By girls," he said and waved.

The girls finished their lunch and Lisa took them home. Since four cars came in while Lisa was at the garage, she could tell that Jonathon was going to be rather busy. She'd wait until he came home to talk with him about what the judge discussed with her. She wanted him to look at the rules with her.

When he came home that evening, she waited until after they all had dinner before she told him about what the judge said. "Well, I guess I'm the new administrator in charge of the orphans or the unwanted children. They'll pay me by the hour and the judge said to put down everything I spent and every mile I went. It appears that if I don't they won't get enough money to fund the program next year. I wonder when we'll get our first child."

"We?" Jonathon asked.

"Yes, we as you have to be part of this too since we'll be bringing children into our home until we find them at home."

"It probably won't be too long but you never know. I just hope that you aren't letting yourself in for some heart aches. Look how easily we both took to our girls when we barely knew them. Just watch out for that, darling."

"I promise I will. But I think the Lord had something to do with our feelings about the girls. I believe that He wanted us to take care of them."

"Darling, I believe that you're right," Jonathon declared.

Chapter Twenty-Four

The New Tenant

The Livingstons headed for church. The girls were all dressed up in their new dresses. They took them to the children's area and headed back to the auditorium to greet a few people. The pastor met them at the door and told them that he needed to talk with them before service.

Jonathon and Lisa followed him into his study. They still had ten minutes before church began.

"You told me that you had a small apartment that you were saving for someone who is in need. Now I suggest you charge this person at least $150 per month. It's a bad policy not to charge something. Mrs. Brewster lost her husband two weeks ago. Her rent is up and she can't afford her present apartment. I believe you know her."

"Yes we do and we would be pleased to let her have the apartment. So she can afford $150 without straining her budget?" Jonathon asked.

"Yes but not a lot more. Now Mrs. Jean Brewster would make a wonderful grandmother for your two daughters. That's something to keep in mind. With Lisa being the new Administrator for the Children's Department, she might need a little time to interview potential parents. And then there's the possibility of you having to keep some of the orphans a day or two. A grandmother would be pretty handy to have there to help you out. Jean Brewster is a worker and a good one."

"That's sound great to me, pastor. But I'd want to watch and see how the girls take to her and how she gets along with them. It would be nice to have someone to leave them with if Jonathon and I both need to be somewhere at the same time and can't take them with us," Lisa replied.

"You mean when you go to the hospital and have this new baby?" the pastor asked.

"How did you know?" Lisa asked.

"I've been around some pregnant ladies and I have four children myself. I hope you get your boy, Jonathon. If it is a girl, when they all grow up, you'll sure be outnumbered."

"That's what I'm afraid of," Jonathon replied.

They all hurried back into the auditorium. They glanced at the pastor as he talked briefly with Jean Brewster. Her sad face suddenly beamed. "It looks as though Jean is rather pleased about renting an apartment from us," Lisa whispered.

Right after the service, Jean came to see them. "The pastor tells me that you'll let me rent the small apartment at your home. May I come see it today and if we agree I'll move in tomorrow? That's the last day they'll let me stay in my present apartment. I have several church people who'll help me move but I need to let them know."

"Follow us home and I'll show you the apartment. It's small, Jean, but it has everything that you need. Lisa lived there and enjoyed it."

Once they arrived at their home, they showed the small apartment to Jean Brewster. "This is perfect. I love it. Would you mind if I did a little painting? I'll pay for the paint."

"Be my guest. Do all the painting you want. Now did you want me to leave the furniture?"

"If you wouldn't mind, Jonathon, I could use it. Now I can pay $200 easily. I think the pastor said something about $150 but that isn't enough. You could rent this for $500 easily and I insist on $200."

"If you insist you may pay $200. Here's the key. Move in when you wish," Jonathon stated.

Shortly after Jonathon went to work the next day, Jean Brewster came to the house and began moving in. She looked so happy. She had wondered what she was going to do. The apartment she had been living in cost way too much money. Without her husband's pay, she'd never be able to afford it and have anything left for utilities and food. This apartment of Jonathon and Lisa's was perfect. She didn't want a big place as she knew that all that room would make it seem lonesome.

Jean was hoping to make friends with Lisa's two girls. It was summer time now and they'd be home all day most days. She would work on making good friends with the two pretty little girls. She knew them from church but would they be as friendly away from church as when they were there? You never knew about children.

When she looked around the apartment she was pleased that it didn't need cleaning. That saved her a lot of time getting settled. Her friends that helped move her had already left and she was putting things away. She couldn't finish it all today but tomorrow was another day.

Jean knocked on the Livingston's door.

"How are you doing, Jean? Are you getting settled all right?" Lisa asked.

"Yes, I'm about half finished and I thought I'd quit for the night. Now I wanted to pay the rent. This is the fifth so I'll pay it now and know that it is due on the fifth of every month."

"Let me give you a receipt, Jean." Lisa hurried and found the book and made out the receipt. Now why don't you have a cup of coffee with me?"

"You don't have to ask me twice," the lady answered.

While they were drinking their coffee the two girls came into the dining room. "Hello, Mrs. Brewster," they both said at the same time and smiled at the lady.

"You girls know Mrs. Brewster?" Lisa asked.

"Yes, she helps in children's church. We have fun with her. All the children call her grandma. Can we call her that at home?" Sabrina asked her mother.

"I don't see why not. Well, grandma, if you need anything, just let me know or let one of the girls know. They can help a lot." She thought it would take a while before the girls got used to Mrs. Brewster but evidently they already knew her better than their parents did. That was nice.

As the days past whenever Lisa needed her, Jean often baby sat the two Livingston girls. She would take nothing for that service. In reality she should be paying a lot more for that apartment so therefore she could help by babysitting.

Jean appeared to love babysitting the two girls and Lisa took advantage of that. Lisa knew that the woman was lonesome and the girls were good company for her. It appeared that Jean had a lot of things for the girls to do in her apartment. There were all sorts of games they could play as well as some clay that they could make vases out of and then bake. The girls loved to visit grandma.

Lisa was able to leave the house and interview some potential parents without taking her girls and that was helpful. Now she had interviewed the first four on Mason's list. They all sounded as though they would make great parents. Virginia Mason at least did something right. Lisa was impressed with the first four parents she interviewed.

It felt good to Lisa to have parents ready to adopt children without having to research the background at the time of the adoption. She made sure she wrote all the mileage down and her time as well. If she didn't and the judge found out about it, she would probably get a good scolding. One thing for sure, Lisa didn't want to keep a baby more than a few hours.

Sabrina was now a third grader and Sissy was in kindergarten. She had some time free during the day. If she wasn't pregnant she'd go work on the vehicles in the garage but she could just hear Jonathon's objection to that. Then when her baby came she sure didn't want to leave the infant with someone else. She'd just have to postpone anymore work in the garage for the time being—probably until she had her family raised.

Jean often asked if the girls could come into her apartment. She wanted to teach them to embroidery and knit and sew. She had a list a mile long for the girls to learn. Lisa let them go. They always came out with some item that they had made and were so proud of it. She noticed that Jean made them do it right.

"I had to tear all the thread out because I didn't do it right," griped Sissy.

"Well, darling, it's good to learn to do things right. Next time you'll do it right and won't have to tear out the thread."

"Yeah, I guess so."

Jean and Lisa had a talk one day.

"Lisa, do you know how much I love your two children? They are so much company for me. They are good and get along so well together. Oh, once in a while they have a fuss but they wouldn't be normal if they didn't. I want to thank you for letting them come to my apartment and visit."

"Let me thank you for teaching them to sew. That's something you could teach me. I never learned to sew. I was too busy helping Jonathon in the garage when I was about eleven and twelve. That was what I liked to do. Sewing was for other girls, not for me."

The two enjoyed their cup of coffee. Lisa knew that they had the right person in that small apartment. Jean didn't seem like an outsider. She seemed like family and her family kept growing.

Chapter Twenty-Five

Interviewing Parents

The first child that needed parents was brought to Lisa's home. They had called and told her that they would bring Troy McAfee to her house at ten o'clock. When they hung up, she immediately called the Gleasons. She asked them to come to her house at ten. Mrs. Gleason told her they would be there. She'd have to go to his work place and pick him up first.

When the officer arrived with the boy who was six months old, Lisa knew that it was a good thing she had called the Gleasons. What a beautiful baby boy he was. She'd like to keep him but she wouldn't even dare try. She would have her third child in a few months and that was enough children in the home. But this boy sure was a keeper. Such a smile he had.

Jensen and Teresa Gleason knocked on the door and Lisa welcomed them in. They took one look at the boy and fell in love with him. "He's beautiful," Teresa remarked.

"He sure is," Jensen agreed.

"His name is Troy. Now, you fill out this paper and then take it to the judge. I will follow you in my car. Once the judge signs the paper, you can take the baby home with you," Lisa informed them.

"We have a car seat. Could Troy ride with us?" Teresa asked.

"I'm afraid that's against the rules. I can't turn him over until the judge signs these papers. It would be good if you could take him as I'm getting a little too attached to him, but I already have two girls. The rules state that the adopting parents can't take the child until the adoption papers are signed. I suppose it's a good rule but even if I disagree with it, I have to follow it."

"We wouldn't want you to break the rules. It looks as though you have a boy on the way," Teresa added and smiled. The woman was very pregnant she thought. It wouldn't be long before she had her own little baby boy.

The group drove to the judge's courtroom. They had to wait some time as the judge was working on a trial. The officer said they would close at eleven for lunch and it was almost that time.

"How did you do, Lisa, when you took the boy in your home? Did you want to keep him?" the officer asked.

"How did you know that? He's a gorgeous boy, but I have two girls and soon will have another child. I have to keep telling myself that. I guess I just love children too much," Lisa remarked.

"Oh, I think children need all the loving they can get," the officer said. "It looks like court is letting out. Wait until everyone leaves the courtroom and then we'll go in," the officer stated.

Once inside the judge welcomed them all. He looked over the papers and signed them. "You have a very good record and Lisa tells me that your house and wages are appropriate. This little one needs lots of love. He doesn't seem to be afraid of strangers and that is good. Now take good care of him," the judge ordered.

"We promise," they both said.

"You may take the boy now."

"Thank you, Judge Watson, for signing the papers and letting us have this good looking chap," Jensen remarked. With that said, the two happy people walked out of the courtroom with the young boy.

"Now where is your paper work, Lisa?"

"Right here, judge." Lisa answered and handed it to him.

"This is very good. Those mileage and hours will help keep this position. I think you have another one coming in about two weeks. He's in the hospital due to an automobile accident. His parents were killed. He wasn't hurt that much but the doctor wanted to keep an eye on him to make sure he didn't have head injury. It was a terrible accident and it's a wonder that the boy survived."

"That's too bad about the parents dying. I'll be waiting for him and in the meantime I'll call the next one on my list," Lisa promised.

"You tell Jonathon if a child comes in while you're in the hospital he has to take care of it. And then tell me what he says," smiled the judge.

"Jonathon would just keep the child and wouldn't look for anyone to adopt the orphan. He fell in love with the girls just looking at them from the kitchen without even talking with them. You think I'm bad, he's worse when it comes to giving up children. He would have had a fit over Troy. He probably would have wanted to keep him. He gave me a lecture on not getting too close when a baby comes up for adoption but I think he was also talking to himself."

"You two are children lovers," the judge said. "I'll see you in two weeks with another child.

When Lisa arrived home, she called the potential parents. She told them that they could have the boy in about a week or two. Somehow she didn't think the hospital would keep the boy the whole two weeks and she wanted the potential parents to be ready.

It was only one week when they called her with another boy. The officer brought him to her house. "His name is Timothy. He's a sweetheart. He's eleven months old and a very bright boy," the officer remarked.

"He's darling," Lisa stated. There was another child she would keep in a minute. Lisa was only glad that she didn't have to keep him over night. If she kept him one night she wouldn't want to give him up.

Jim and June Smith arrived at the house all smiles. Jim lifted the boy up and looked at him and received a big smile for it. He hugged the infant. It didn't take much to know that the man was going to love his son.

Lisa explained what they had to do.

"Can we take the boy in our car," asked June.

"I'm sorry but I can't release him until the judge signs this paper. I see you filled it out properly. Now I'll meet you there."

Once again the judge smiled. "You're doing very well, Lisa, two children in ten days. Now how are you handling this?"

"I would have loved to keep both boys. If you ever find someone who wants this position, let me know. My heart goes out to those children so much. If I had to keep them overnight, I don't think I could give them up."

"I was afraid of that. The reason I asked is that I know a woman who needs a job. Her husband died. I've known this woman all my life and she's a good lady. Do you want to quit and let her have the position?" the judge asked.

"Yes, I do. It's just too heartbreaking for me."

"You're a softy, my dear."

"I know," Lisa agreed.

"Turn in your paper work and you'll receive your wages. Bring back what you have and the list of prospective parents. One thing you don't need is stress with you being pregnant. Now if you weren't so attached to every child you see, it wouldn't hurt you so much."

"Silly, isn't it?" she asked.

"No, it just shows that you are a caring woman. But I'd like to keep your name incase some time Mrs. Lawson can't do the job for some reason. She does like to visit with her children in another state. So if you wouldn't mind, I'd like to call you when and if I ever need help," the judge explained.

"That's fine with me, Judge Watson. Anytime you need me, give me a call and I'll help except when I'm in the hospital having my baby."

"You'll have a fine boy, Lisa. Take good care of him."

"A boy would sure please Jonathon. He wants one so much but if we have a pretty little girl, he wouldn't care."

"You'll have a boy," the judge remarked.

"Here's hoping."

Lisa left with a smile. She sure liked the judge. He was definitely a people person who cared about what happened in other people's lives. He was a good and an honest judge.

She was glad that she had the experience with the two boys but Lisa was more than pleased that she didn't have to adopt out another child. In her home were two beautiful girls that she was very proud of and they were enough for now.

Chapter Twenty-Six

The New Comer

Lisa was getting pretty good size now. It wasn't the easiest thing to get up out of the easy chair. It wouldn't be too long before the baby would be born. According to Jean she was going to have a boy. She rather hoped the lady was right. Jonathon sure wanted a boy. But she knew him and he'd love a girl too. He liked kids but it appeared that most men wanted at least one boy.

A week later, Lisa woke up with pains at midnight. She got out of bed and walked around. The pains seemed to be about fifteen minutes apart. That would mean there wouldn't be too much of a rush but she wanted to go to the hospital now. She could just envision having that child in an automobile.

She woke up Jonathon and he couldn't figure out why she was up in the middle of the night. "Go back to sleep dear, it's only two thirty in the morning."

"All right but then you have to deliver the baby if you don't want to take me to the hospital," Lisa remarked with a silly grin.

Jonathon jumped out of bed and slipped on his jeans and grabbed her suitcase and was ready to go.

"Jonathon, I'd rather you had a shirt on instead of your pajama tops. I think it would look better since we'll be in a public hospital."

Embarrassed, Jonathon quickly changed his shirt and escorted his moaning wife to the vehicle and took off. The girls were spending the night with grandma. Every now and then she had to have a sleepover with them and they loved it. He'd call her later and let her know that they were at the hospital.

He looked up at her window and she was waving goodbye. Jean Brewster didn't miss much. She had a feeling that today was the day that Lisa would have that baby boy and she was right. She had heard the movement in their apartment and heard them go outside and that could mean only one thing—they were headed for the hospital.

Jonathon started to the hospital but every groan his wife groaned, he speeded up another five miles an hour. Lisa thought she had plenty of time but the pains were coming five minutes apart now. She was pleased that Jean knew they were leaving as she was so excited about the baby coming she completely forgot to tell her.

Jonathon went with Lisa into the delivery room. He watched the baby as it came into the world. One nurse looked at the man and decided she'd better bring him a chair. He was just a little pale and wide-eyed. Jonathon knew it was a miracle to have a baby but to witness it was something else. He gladly sat down in the chair that the nurse provided. He did feel a little week-kneed after witnesses the birth of his son.

He stayed with his wife until they moved her from the delivery room to a room that would be hers for a day or two. He now had a son, a good looking baby boy. Lisa was back in her room and resting. Jonathon stayed for some time and then remarked, "I need to go to the garage and explain to Joseph why I didn't open the garage this morning. I'll see you later tonight," he promised and kissed her goodbye. "By the way, thanks for my son, Justin Jonathon Livingston, I do believe that he's a keeper."

Lisa smiled. She loved the infant and could hardly wait to take him home to the girls. They would be thrilled.

Jonathon stopped by the house and told Jean about his new son and then headed for the garage. He knew that his workers would already be at the garage and he needed to be there with them. He didn't get much sleep but he did get a son. He thought if he kept remembering his son that would keep him awake most of the day.

Jean was so pleased for Jonathon and Lisa. Jonathon had his son and the labor was over for Lisa. She would probably be coming home tomorrow. The doctors didn't keep the ladies as long now days as they did in her time. She spent five days in the hospital with her children. Sometimes in today's world they let the mothers go home the next day after the child was born. That was much too soon as far as she was concerned. Mother's needed a rest time and the only way they would get it was to stay in the hospital.

Jonathon had asked her to get lunch for the children and to do so in his kitchen. "Make what ever you like. And thanks!"

The girls and Jean had their lunch and just finished the dishes when the doorbell rang. Jean was always cautious of strangers so she didn't open the screen door.

"Hello, may I help you?" she asked.

"I've come for my grandchildren. I understand you have them here. The judge said I could have them because I'm their only relative."

"Let me see your warrant or papers." Jean asked and turned to Sabrina and mouthed, "Call 911."

"The judge said I didn't need any papers. Now just let me have the girls and there'll be no trouble."

"You can't have the children without some paper work and certainly not without talking to their mom and dad. They are both gone now but should be home most any time." Jean tried to stall him as much as she could. She knew that Sabrina would ask the police to come. The girl had a frightened look on her face when the man demanded that they turn the girls over to him.

"Now if I have to come back with the judge, he's going to be very mad and probably will arrest you and put you in jail. Do you want that to happen?" the stranger asked.

"No, I don't want to go to jail. The Livingstons have had these girls for four years now. I believe it will take a court fight for you to take the children away from them."

"That's not what the judge said. You're asking for a jail sentence, lady. Why don't you just cooperate and save yourself some time in jail?"

"Then I'll just have to go to jail because your not getting my granddaughters," she stated firmly.

"Your granddaughters," he repeated.

About that time two police vehicles drove in one in front and one in back of the man's automobile. Sergeant Anderson walked up to the door with his gun in his hand ready to fire it if necessary.

"Now what's the problem here?" he asked.

"This man is trying to take Sabrina and Sissy. He says he's their grandfather," Jean stated.

"Well, he looks like that kidnapper that is on one of the wanted posters in the police station as well as the post office. That's what he looks like. Now since the girls' grandfathers on both sides of the family passed away years ago, I don't think this man is telling you the truth, Mrs. Brewster. What do you think?"

"I think the man told a bold face lie," Jean stated and stared at the man.

"I'm not that man on the wanted poster. He may look like me, but I'm not a kidnapper," the stranger stated.

"Well, you just tried to kidnap these two girls. I'd say you were very much a kidnapper." He handcuffed the stranger and put him in the police vehicle of the other policeman. The second policeman drove him to the station.

"Where's Sabrina?" Sergeant Anderson asked.

"Here," Sabrina answered.

"You did a good job when you telephoned the police. I'm very proud of you and I'll tell your father what a good job you did," Sergeant Anderson promised the girl.

The sergeant left and headed for Jonathon's garage. He informed him what happened and emphasized how good Sabrina explained the problem to the police. You have a smart gal there, Jonathon."

"I know Sabrina is an intelligent girl. I can't imagine why some guy came after those two. In the back of my mind I keep wondering if this was getting even time. I wonder if Mrs. Mason had anything to do with this. That's terrible to say but she was awful mad when she had to go to prison. She threw daggers at me with her eyes as if to say she would get even."

"Well, I don't know but I suggest that you keep your doors locked in the day time and someone be with the girls while they are outside playing. Let's not take anymore chances."

Jonathon agreed. He sure hated to tell Lisa what happened. He wondered if she ever said anything to the girls about not going with strangers or talking with strangers. Perhaps he'd have a talk with them tonight. If Mrs. Mason had anything to do with it, she wouldn't stop at one try. She'd have her companions try again. He often wondered how the city had ever hired her in that position. The woman didn't like children. But something she said must have impressed them. Mrs. Mason was a pretty good actress.

Jonathon took a few hours the next day to talk with the judge. He wondered if the official might have found out something more about Virginia Mason.

As he entered the courtroom, no one was there except the Judge Watson. "Well, Jonathon, I expected you to come talk to me. I'm sorry what that man tried to do to get your children but he's in jail and it's unlikely that he'll ever get out. I do have some news for you. It appears that Mrs. Mason was involved in more than overcharging on adoption fees. She connected with the gang which has invaded our town."

"Well, I figured she had to have someone on the outside to try to take the children. Was this man also from the gang?"

"That man has so many things against him that I can't even remember them all. Yes, he's part if the group and he's well acquainted with Mrs. Mason. One of the guards caught the woman sending a message with her visitor, another man that we figure is a gang member. Somehow she's still running things behind bars. You keep those girls close with you. Don't let them play outside alone. Tell them never to go with a stranger no matter what they say to them."

"You can count on that. School will start before too long and I need the teachers to know not to let my children go home with anyone but me."

"That's a wise idea. Tell the principal that as well. Say congratulations on that boy. I hear he was born yesterday. How's he doing?"

"I'm taking him home today. I can hardly wait to get my hands on my son. I ordered a boy and got a good looking one," Jonathon answered.

"Well, take good care of him and bring him by one day so I can see what he looks like. I'll bet he's a keeper."

"That he is," Jonathon remarked with a proud grin.

He wondered how the girls would be with Justin. They would probably think he belonged to them and want to do everything for him.

Jonathon left. He'd have another talk with his children, wife and their "grandmother" to emphasize watching them carefully. If Virginia Mason was getting information out, she'll keep her promise about getting even with them. The woman was vicious.

He hoped that somehow they'd be able to find out who all was taking her messages. They put an order on monitoring her phone calls because of the attempt to kidnap the two girls. Jonathon sure hope that would put an end to it but he knew she had frequent visitors.

Well, he had to go bring his wife home. The doctor said about four in the afternoon he could pick her and Justin up. That worked for him. He didn't get too much time in at the garage but the work appeared to get done anyway. He had two very good workers. He knew when he wasn't there, the two worked over time to catch up on any vehicles they possible could. They never mentioned the overtime to him, though. That was two men who enjoyed being mechanics.

He entered the hospital and headed for Lisa's room. She was all packed, had her son in her arms and was ready to leave the hospital. She wanted to take her baby home.

"You aren't a little anxious to show off your boy are you?" Jonathon asked her with a grin.

"Am I ready to take him home and show him to grandma? Yes I am. He's so beautiful, Jonathon. Look at him. How can someone love one so quickly? He's our boy."

"He sure is. He's a keeper. Now they are bringing a wheel chair for you. Do you want to hold the suitcase while I carry the baby?" Jonathon asked with a teasing grim. He knew he wouldn't get away with that.

"I think I'll hold the baby."

And she did.

Chapter Twenty-Seven

The Uncle

There was a lot of excitement when Lisa came home from the hospital with Justin Jonathon Livingston. The girls couldn't keep their hands off of him. They wanted to hold him constantly and argued whose turn it was to hold him.

"Now, girls, the baby has to lie down and sleep sometimes and mamma has to feed him sometimes. You can't hold him all the time. Now we'll take turns. Sissy held him last time and when he wakes up, Sabrina can hold him unless he wakes up hungry. We have to remember whose turn it is to hold Justin."

"When do I get my turn," asked Grandma Brewster.

"Well, what about me, don't I get a turn," Jonathon asked.

"One thing for sure, I'm glad I am nursing him and that way I get my turn at holding him. Now girls, see how many people you have to share him with. Justin is going to get a lot of attention but I don't want him held all day long. You'll spoil him and when you go back to school he'll want me to hold him all the time."

"That's okay, I'll be here and I'll hold him," teased Jean smiling at Lisa.

"I have no hopes for the boy to be anything except spoiled. Now, no more fighting girls and you two grownups that goes for you too," Lisa remarked.

"Yes ma'am," Jean agreed.

"Yes, I understand," Jonathon answered.

The girls laughed. They knew they were just teasing them. Sabrina decided that she should be more grownup than to fight over the baby but he was so much fun to hold. She could hardly wait for him to smile at her.

School would begin tomorrow so that evening Jonathon had a talk with the household. "Sabrina and Sissy, I'd like you to listen to daddy. You're never to leave the school with anyone except your mother, father or grandma—just us three and no one else."

"Why, daddy?"

Leave it to Sissy to ask the whys. "Because we have a woman that doesn't like us and although she is in prison, she'll likely try to send someone to kidnap you. Now will you promise me never to get in the car with anyone else?"

"We promise," both girls replied. They couldn't imagine anyone wanting to kidnap them. But after Sabrina had called 911 she began to think that just maybe someone would. She would be careful and make sure Sissy was too.

"It doesn't matter what they say. They could say they were your uncle, brother, a policeman or anything but you still don't get into the car with them. They might even tell you that we've been hurt. Then what would you do?"

"We won't get in the car. We'll wait at school until you to come for us," Sabrina promised. "Isn't that right, Sissy?"

Sissy said yes.

Two months after school started, Lisa went to pick up the children. There was Sissy but she could see Sabrina no where. "Sissy, where is Sabrina?"

"I don't know," she answered.

The teachers were outside watching the children until they were picked up by their parents. Lisa walked over to Sabrina's teacher and asked her where her daughter was. "I don't see Sabrina anywhere on the playground. Mrs. Evens, where is Sabrina."

"Oh, her uncle came to get her."

"Mrs. Evens, you were told never to release our girls to anyone but us and Jean Brewster. Did you not understand that?"

"Well, it was her uncle..." Mrs. Evans repeated.

"She doesn't have an uncle." Lisa was mad. She picked up the phone and called 911. "My daughter has been abducted."

When the police interviewed Mrs. Evens, they talk rough with her. "You have in your possession a statement that says you're never to release these girls to anyone except three people. Now why have you broken that trust? You know I can put you in jail for what you did."

Mrs. Evens broke down and sobbed. "The man said he would kill my children if I didn't let him have the girl. I didn't know what to do. He had a gun pointed in my back. He had called me out of the room and said he needed to talk with me. He left the class room door open and I think some of the children could see what was going on. What could I do but go along with him? He would have shot me and perhaps some of the children. There was nothing I could do except let him take Sabrina away with him. The girl didn't argue but followed him."

"Why didn't you call the police?"

"He said she would kill my family if I told anyone. Now he'll probably do that," she sobbed.

"How long ago was that?"

"About half an hour ago," Mrs. Evans informed him.

"Did you notice the vehicle he was driving? Did you look out the window?"

"He was driving a Chevrolet about ten years old, I'd guess. I deliberately watched him put the girl in the car. Are you going to protect my family?"

"I'll send a policeman to your home," promised the sergeant.

Sergeant Larson made a call to the station. "Send a helicopter and look for a Chevrolet approximately tens years old. We don't know what direction the kidnapper was headed so you might send out two helicopters. The Livingston girl named Sabrina has been kidnapped."

In the meantime, Sabrina was talking with her abductor. "So you're my uncle. I'm surprised. We didn't know anything about our relatives." Sabrina had watched a program where the girl went along with the kidnapper and won over his faith in her so she thought she would try that. In the program the girl had escaped from her abductor. Perhaps it would work with this man.

"I'm sure hungry, uncle. Can we stop and have something to eat pretty soon?" she asked.

"Yes, my niece, we shall stop up here a little ways." Winfred was so pleased that the girl believed his story. He wouldn't have any problems with her. He was pleased that he didn't have to tie her up and gag her to keep her quiet.

"After we eat we shall go to the next town and I'll buy you some gifts. I couldn't do that before because I didn't know where you were."

"That's nice but you don't have to do that. You're a nice man," Sabrina exclaimed.

The waitress brought their meals and Sabrina ate even though she didn't feel like it. When she finished, she asked if he could order her some ice cream with chocolate on it. He agreed.

"I'm going to the bathroom and I'll be right back so I can eat my ice cream." She kissed the man on the cheek and said thanks.

Boy, it sure didn't take long to win this girl over to my side. She must not get much attention at home as she sure eating up what little attention he give her. He waited until the waitress came with the bills. He asked for a small dish of ice cream with chocolate on it. She took the bill back to adjust it.

The kitchen and the bathrooms were in the same direction. When Sabrina reached the bathroom, she noticed that her abductor wasn't watching her. She quickly slipped into the kitchen.

"I'm Sabrina Livingston and the man I'm with has kidnapped me from my school. Could you call my parents and let them know that I'm here and they'll come and take me home."

"How do we know you're telling us the truth," asked the cook.

"Just call this number and tell them and you'll find out," she suggested.

One of the kitchen workers called the number. "Is this the Livingston home?" she asked.

"Yes, do you know anything about my granddaughter, Sabrina Livingston? She's been kidnapped and the police are out looking for her."

"She's hiding in my kitchen. I work at the restaurant on the corner Cherry Street and Elm Street."

"I'll get a hold of the parents right away. Please keep her out of sight. The kidnapper is very smart and he'd talk you into turning her over to him. He would convince you that she was lying but she's telling you the truth. Please keep her hidden and away from that kidnapper."

"She's hiding in the closet now," the worker assured the grandmother.

The kidnapper came into the kitchen after waiting around fifteen minutes. "Have you seen my niece? She went to the bathroom and never came back. I'm worried about her."

"She's not in the kitchen. Perhaps you should look in other booths where she might have found some friend and is visiting with them. You can never tell what children will do. Why don't you look outside?" The cook looked at the man. He had seen that man's picture on the wall of the post office. "I hope you find her. Kids can be a lot of worry."

The abductor walked away. He had searched the whole restaurant and the girl was no where to be found. He went outside and looked around. Unless she was hiding in the bushes, she wasn't outside. He had a good thing going and now he had failed. The boss wasn't going to like that. Perhaps he'd stick around a little longer and see if she might just be playing in the yard somewhere. He sat in his car and watched carefully for some sign of the girl.

He saw two men drive up. One went into the restaurant and the other one stayed in the car. Must be going to get a take-out lunch he assumed. He liked to watch people so that's what he did while waiting for Sabrina to show up.

In the restaurant, Sergeant Larson headed for the kitchen. He was dressed in plain clothes as he didn't want the abductor to flee at the sight of a policeman. He went into the kitchen and showed his badge and asked if Sabrina Livingston was there.

Sabrina came out of the closet grinning. "Hello, sergeant, I'm sure glad to see you. I went along with the man who took me until I had a chance to escape. He thought I really considered him my uncle. Did you catch him?"

"He's out in his automobile and my partner and I are going to do that right now. Stay here until I come for you."

Sabrina stayed.

Once outside, the two policemen arrested the kidnapper and put him in the police vehicle.

"What are you arresting me for? I haven't done anything wrong," he stated. "Now take these cuffs off of me."

"We're arresting you for kidnapping," Larsen replied.

"I don't have a child with me so how can you arrest me for kidnapping? You can't prove a thing," he grumbled.

"Well, there is a teacher who will testify how you threatened her if she didn't let you take Sabrina. And then there is Sabrina in the restaurant that pointed you out as the kidnapper. There is a school class room of children who'll give the same testimony," the sergeant explained.

The abductor said nothing more. He knew he was caught. That little snip of a girl was pretending all along. He thought she was a little too enthusiastic for someone who was kidnapped. There was no way he was going to get out of this kidnapping. He should never have trusted the girl. If he had tied her up and gagged her, he would have accomplished his task. Now he was headed for prison and he knew as soon as they saw his record, it would be for a good long time.

One policeman drove to the police station and delivered the prisoner. He had said nothing all the time that he was in the police car. He would have an attorney but it wasn't going to do him any good.

The other one took Winfred's automobile and drove Sabrina home in it.

After the policemen finished delivering their passengers both of them headed for the school. They knew that Mrs. Evens was waiting for some news. They wanted to let her know that Sabrina was home and hurt in no way.

Mrs. Evens saw them as they came into the school. Now what, she wondered. In all her years of teaching, nothing like this ever happened. She knew she could be arrested but what was she to do, refuse and get shot. Let her family be shot. To her she didn't have any choice but to do what she did.

School had been out for some time but Mrs. Evans stayed waiting for news about Sabrina. Sergeant Larson came over to her and said, "Mrs. Evens, we just want to let you know that the kidnapper has been caught and Sabrina has been returned to her home. All is well. The man who kidnapped her has a lot of charges against him including murder. There is no way he can do anything to you or your family. He was under the direction of a member of a gang in this town. We're trying to arrest all of them but it's hard to do that until they commit a crime and by that time someone usually gets hurt. We need to catch one who will tell all in a plea bargain.

Mrs. Even sat down. That was one big relief! "Thank you so much for telling me. I appreciate it very much. I'm sorry that I let her go but I think she saw the gun and that was why she was willing to go with the man. She had heard about school shootings before. She's a smart girl."

"That I agree with. Do you know that she made the kidnapper think that she really believed that he was her uncle? When he began to trust her, that's when she slipped away. That girl was cool as a cucumber." The policemen left laughing.

Chapter Twenty-Eight

Sabrina Mentions her Mother

When Sabrina returned home her father questioned her. "Why did you go with that man that was a stranger? You know you aren't to have anything to do with someone you don't know. Why would you ever get in his car?"

"Because I could see the gun he was holding on the teacher. I though he might shoot her and a bunch of children to get to me, so I went with him. I pretended to believe that he was my uncle and went along with everything he said. Then I told him I was hungry so he stopped at the restaurant and we ate dinner. I asked for an ice cream dish with chocolate and then told him I had to go to the bathroom. But instead I went to the kitchen and told them I was kidnapped and asked them to call my home."

"How did you know enough to go along with the man? What made you think of that?" Jonathon asked.

"Remember that movie we saw a week ago? The girl went along with her kidnapper and she was able to slip away. So I thought I would try that. I called him uncle and I even kissed him on the cheek so he would really think that I believed him," Sabrina explained.

Jonathon just shook his head. He didn't realize she was old enough to think this out. She was a brave girl to go with the man to prevent him from shooting the teacher or any of the children. Very likely if he had done that, he would have taken Sabrina anyway and this whole situation would have come out totally different. He was pleased that she saw that movie. You just never know about your children or what they are capable of. He was proud of his daughter and her ability to think things through.

He needed to go back to the garage and finish up for the day. He sure hoped this was the last incident. They had lived in such a good town until that gang came. Perhaps even yet they will catch all the members.

Lisa came over and hugged her daughter. "You're one smart girl. I'm so proud of you. I think you're right that if you didn't go with him the man would have shot someone to force you to. You were very brave, darling. I hope you never have to go through that again."

One thing for sure, they would be out in the yard with the children. It seems there was no end to Mrs. Mason revenge. Hopefully, they'll recommend her be placed in solitary confinement where she would have no contact with anyone.

The year went by quickly. School was almost out. Sabrina would be a fifth grader next year and Sissy a third grader. The girls had grown a lot since she first took them home.

There were no more incidents the past year. Justin was growing up. Lisa almost hated to seem him get older. He was so much fun as a baby. Just watching him go through all the stages that children go through as they grow was enjoyable. She had missed those stages with the girls. Sabrina was ten years old now. Her mother looked at her. She was growing into a beautiful girl. She would have to watch out for the boys when Sabrina got a little older. Sometimes the girl acted a little more grownup than she should be for her age.

One day Sabrina went to find her mother. "Mom, I want to talk with you about my birth mother. I would like to find her and make sure she's alright."

Lisa was shocked. She stared at her daughter not quite knowing what to say. Where on earth did this come from? The past six years she had never mentioned her mother. Very gently she talked to the girl. "Sabrina, your mother died in a car accident, remember. That's when you came to live with me."

"No, she didn't die. The policeman told me that she'd be all right. They were going to take her to the hospital. He told me that he'd find a home for Sissy and me," Sabrina stated the information as if there wasn't any doubt in her mind but that it was true.

"I could take you to her grave," Lisa offered. How was she going to convince Sabrina that her mother had died in that accident?

"Well, it may have her name on it but she isn't in the grave," Sabrina stated definitely without the least bit of doubt.

"I just don't know what to say to you. The policeman told me that your mother was killed in the accident. That's all I know, dear. I didn't even know when the funeral was so I couldn't go or take you girls. Perhaps if you had gone to the funeral you would remember."

"Would you take me to talk with the policeman who was at the accident? He can tell you that she's still alive." Sabrina looked at her mother. Why did the policeman tell her that she had died but told Sabrina that she was alive? Was the girl just wishing or was it true?

"We'll wait until your father comes home and we'll talk with him. Since school is out, we could go talk to Sergeant Larson perhaps tomorrow. Would that be all right?" Lisa asked her determined daughter. She'd never seen Sabrina like this before. The thing that worried her was that the girl usually knew what happened when she stated something so definite.

"Sabrina, what made you think about your mother after all this time?"

"I've been having dreams about her. I didn't mention her before because I didn't want Sissy and me to go back to living in a car and have to drive away in a hurry when someone was following us."

"How long had you lived in the car?" Lisa asked.

"About three months, I think. We were at some nice house when my mom saw somebody was looking for her and she hurried us away. She had terrible headaches and took a lot of medicine and some of it affected her mind I think."

Now the story seemed more plausible that the birth mother might be alive and that's the reason that the policeman told me that the mother had been killed in the automobile accident. How did Sabrina remember all that? The mother was likely a witness to some criminal act and the criminals knew it.

All these years and Sabrina knew about her mother being alive and didn't say a word. She now believed what Sabrina told her. Lisa had never caught her in a lie even when she got into a little trouble at the house. Sabrina always admitted that she was the one that broke the glass or whatever she did wrong. Therefore Lisa believed her story about her birth mother.

When Jonathon came home Lisa had everyone eat an early dinner. She wanted to have a talk with him. No, she wanted Sabrina to have a talk with her father and see what he thought about her story.

After dinner was over they went into the living room and sat down. "Now, Sabrina, your mother tells me that you need to talk with me because you have some information on your mother that we don't know about."

Sabrina began to tell him how the policeman told her that her mother was going to be all right but that she and Sissy had to live with someone else. She told him how they had left a nice safe house because her mother was afraid of someone. When Sabrina was through with her story, she looked at her dad.

"Can we talk with Sergeant Larson about my birth mother?" she asked.

"Yes, but I have to make an appointment. I'm going to see if the sergeant can come over to our house and talk with us here. Sabrina, how come you never mentioned your mother before now?"

"I didn't want to go back to living in a car. You had such a nice house and we had plenty to eat. My birth mother didn't have much money and we didn't get much to eat. She had to beg for food."

"I see. Well, tomorrow is Friday and I'll call the sergeant. Perhaps we can invite him over for dinner. What do you think, Mamma, can we have a guest for dinner?" Jonathon asked.

"I don't see why not. If you were to find your mother, would you want to go back and live with her," Jonathon asked the question cautiously. He would hate to lose these two girls. Legally, they couldn't take them but if the girls insisted…

"No, I want to live with you and mamma. I just want to make sure she's okay and has food and has someone to take care of her. I keep dreaming bad dreams about her," Sabrina explained.

"Well, you two get dressed for bed and if you want to watch your favorite program tonight, you do that and then it will be bedtime."

The girls hurried up the stairs and soon came down in their pajamas all ready to watch their favorite program. He left them alone and went into the kitchen to help Lisa with the dishes.

"That is some story your daughter told," he remarked.

"I know. I tried so hard to convince her that her mother had died in the accident and she wouldn't accept that. She appeared to know it wasn't true, but the sergeant told me that she had been killed. I wanted to take her to her mother's grave but she said even if there was a grave with her name on it, she wouldn't be there. She's a determined girl, Jonathon. We have to look into this," Lisa exclaimed.

"If this is confidential information, the sergeant may not be able to tell us anything. But wait till Sabrina attacks him and he'll tell her something." Jonathon laughed. "That girl had a way of getting things out of you."

"I was sure stunned when she brought the subject up. Now I hope that she can find her mother if indeed she's still alive. It would be nice for the girls to see her and get to know her again. I wonder what Sergeant Larson will tell us. I'm a little upset with him telling me she was killed when it appears she wasn't."

"Lisa, we don't know what the truth is. If he was told to tell you that, he had no choice in the matter. We have to talk with him and give him a chance to explain. I think that he'll tell us the truth and we'll have to keep it quiet if the mother is some type of witness or something. If they were living in a nice place and then moved because the mother was afraid, that sounds like someone was after her. I wonder what happened to her father and if this has anything to do with him?"

"I don't know but I sure want to find out. I think she said her father died. I remember her telling me that he was mean to them and often hit them and their mother. I'll make a good meal and bribe Sergeant Larson into telling us all about the children's mother," Lisa stated laughing.

"Yeah, you do that."

"You don't think my cooking could bribe anyone into telling me what I want to know? I'm hurt to the quick." Lisa laughed.

"I think your cooking could bribe someone but not if they had orders not to tell us anything. The shame would be if they decided to tell Sabrina that she was mistaken about all of it. There would be one upset little girl then."

"I agree," Lisa said. "I sure hope they don't decide that is the best thing to do. Sabrina needs to know the truth."

"I agree with you but what is the truth? I have an idea when we talk with the sergeant, he'll have to go talk with whoever is in charge. Then he'll come back and tell us what he's been told to tell us."

"I just hope it's the truth this time. Oh, I hear Justin fussing. I think he's calling for his father so you better go get him."

"I'd be pleased to go see my boy. He's growing and all in all he's a pretty good kid. I do believe he's a keeper."

Chapter Twenty-Nine

Where was Emma Brothers?

When Jonathon called Sergeant Larson and invited him to dinner, he told him what he wanted to talk to him about. He told him that Sabrina said that her birth mother didn't die in the automobile accident that she only went to the hospital to get medical help for her wounds. Not mincing any words, he told the sergeant he wanted to know the details of the accident.

"I'll be at your house for dinner this evening, Jonathon, but first I have to get clearance to tell you exactly what happened." Larson had been afraid that one day Sabrina would remember that her mother didn't die and he'd have this problem on his hands. If the woman had only stayed in the safe house, she wouldn't have been found and she could have raised her own children. But she thought she saw the man who was after her and she fled. That was the worse thing she could have done. But people don't always think straight when they're in a situation as she was.

The sergeant hated facing the Livingstons. He had been forced to lie to Lisa because that was his orders. They even had a cemetery plot with the mother's name on it. The papers ran the obituary. They wanted the one who was after her to think that she was killed in an accident.

Larson went to talk to the chief. He told him what the problem was. "Now, I'm not going to lie to Lisa and Jonathon again. You can come to dinner and lie to them or I'm going to tell them the truth. I could see the need at the time and it seemed the best thing to do to let them think the mother was dead, but I can see no harm in telling them the truth now."

"I don't know…"

"Are you going to go to the home and lie to them?" Larson asked. "Because I'm sure not going to. I don't care who orders me to," he remarked defiantly.

"No, but I have to call someone to get permission. We never did catch Ted Southerland. There's still a threat out there. I don't think that Emma Brothers should go to the Livingston home if we do decide to tell them. I think that the Livingstons should go on vacation if the girl insists on seeing her mother. Then they can take the girls to see Emma. But we have to have the permission from the ones who are in control of this mission."

"I really never thought that Sabrina would remember anything. But she was five years old but still… She's a clever girl. When she was kidnapped she managed to fool the kidnapper into thinking she believed he was her uncle. The girl isn't dumb. It's just that why now? Why not earlier? The Livingstons said that the two girls never once mentioned their mother all those six years."

"I'll tell you one thing, Chief, you better not try to lie to Sabrina. She'll know if you're lying."

"I imagine she would. I'll talk with you before the day is over and let you know what they say. I'm hoping they'll let us tell the Livingstons and ask them not to repeat the information. That's what I'm hoping."

"Just let me know before I go have dinner with the Livingstons. I don't want to go and eat a good steak dinner and have to tell them I'm sorry I can't talk to you about it. You have to convince those people that Jonathon and Lisa are people who know how to keep their mouths closed. And then you have to get the little girl not to tell anyone. That will be the hard part." Larson went back to his desk and to work.

It might not be so hard to get Sabrina to keep quiet. She would understand the need for that. He'd be glad when the day was over and he had permission to tell all to the Livingstons. First he'd have to apologize for lying to Lisa in the first place and hope they'd understand why he had to.

When he saw the chief come toward him just before closing time, he saw the grin on his face. That was a good sign.

"Well, Larson, tell whatever you need to because you have permission to do that. I had to do a lot of arguing but they finally agreed that the secret shouldn't be kept from the Livingstons. They said if the girls wanted to see their mother, they could but only under police escort. The family would have to go with the police to see Mrs. Emma Brothers," the chief told him.

"Thank you, sir. That's good news. I can enjoy my steak now," Sergeant Larson remarked smiling.

"How do you know it will be steak?" the chief asked.

"Steak dinner is what you bribe people with and I'm going to be bribed to tell all," a smiling sergeant replied.

The chief shook his head and left. He was relieved. He didn't know what they would do if the ones in charge had said no. The Livingstons already believed Sabrina's story and they would make a search to find the mother and perhaps cause danger to the girls and to the mother. This way was much better.

After work, he headed for the Livingston home. He liked the idea of being with that family. He wanted to see the little boy again—Justin that was the boy's name. He was growing up as well as the girls.

He knocked on the door and was invited in. He looked at the toddler. He was two years old if he remembered right. He sure was a cute boy. Larson went over and picked up the boy.

"Do you remember me, Justin?" he asked.

Justin stared at him. Finally he said, "No."

The sergeant laughed. "He's sure a nice looking boy," he told the parents.

"The food is on the table and we're just waiting for you to come in. We wanted to eat first and then we can have a talk. I really think that Sabrina should be in on the talk but if you insist that she shouldn't…"

"She needs to hear what I have to say. But I think the sister ought to visit her grandmother. She's too young to not tell what she knows."

Lisa readily agreed. Knowing Sissy's personality, she knew the girl would tell anyone she talked with. She would never be able to keep a secret. They sat around the table, prayed and then ate. It was a steak dinner just like he wanted and it was delicious. He knew that Lisa was a good cook and always looked forward to eating with them. Being an old bachelor, he enjoyed a good home cooked meal every now and then.

After dinner, Jean came and asked Sissy to keep her company and they would put a puzzle together.

"Can Sabrina come too?" Sissy asked.

"After she finishes a few things that she needs to do. But you and I get to put the first pieces together. How do you like that? We can have a lot of it put together by the time she comes in to help us."

"Okay," Sissy said and followed Jean into her apartment.

Everyone sat down in the family room. Lisa had poured some coffee for the adults and they were ready to hear what the sergeant would tell them.

"First, Lisa, let me apologize for lying to you when the accident happened. I had my orders and had to follow them," he remarked.

"That's okay, as a policeman you have to follow orders. You're forgiven but don't ever do it again," Lisa grinned.

"Now what Sabrina has told you is true. Her mother didn't die. She went to the hospital and stayed in a secluded room. She wasn't hurt that much but had some bruises and scratches and a terrible headache. Emma Brothers told us that the man deliberately ran into her car hoping to kill her. He drove off quickly before anyone could get his license plate.

"Emma was so frightened and knew her children would be in danger so she asked if we would find a good family for them. She signed the papers for them to be adopted out. She figured that sooner or later the man would find her and kill the whole family and she couldn't let that happen. The mother wanted to protect her children and she would rather give them up than take a chance on someone coming after all of them.

"John Brothers wasn't a good man and owed a lot of money to some people who set a deadline for him to pay his debt. When he missed a few deadlines and they realized they weren't going to get paid, they shot him. Emma saw who killed him. They were all part of the gang that moved into town. Emma gave us a very good description of the man. She told the sketch artist and he drew a good picture. I recognized him. It was Ted Southerland, but we could never find him even though we had an all points bulletin out on him.

"Now, if the girls wish to see their mother, they have to go with a police escort. We have a van and you could all go. But we have to set it up and make an appointment. It would be good for Emma to see the children. She knows that they are in a good home and that they are happy. That's what she wanted. She doesn't want to take them back because she could never provide for them. Emma is only pleased that you're taking good care of her girls. I think she'll stay where she is as it's about the last place the gang would look for her. She has a job and is doing very well."

"I would like to see my mother. I'm glad that she is doing well and that she wants to leave us here with mom and dad," Sabrina stated firmly.

"Well, young lady, I shall make the appointment and you shall be escorted by the police. We'll take the whole family. Your birth mother has often asked about you but she knew you were so much better off and would be safer if you stayed with the Livingstons. She doesn't know the name of the people who adopted you. I think it would be best if you didn't tell her that."

"Why?"

"Sabrina, you never know what will happen in the future. Say that fellow that was after her found her and wanted to punish her by coming after her children. They might try to force her to tell who adopted you two girls. Right now she has no idea who adopted her children."

"Okay, that makes sense," Sabrina agreed.

"Sabrina, when you see your mother, you be real careful. Sissy is young and she won't understand that she can't talk about her mother. It would be best if she didn't know that Emma Brothers was her mother."

"I won't tell her," Sabrina promised.

Jonathon didn't say anything but things had to make sense to Sabrina before she would agree to go along with what the officer told her.

"Now are there any questions from anyone?"

"Sissy might say something about her last name is now Livingston. Do you want me to tell her not to do that?" Sabrina asked.

"I think that would be a very good idea. She might listen to you more than she would any one else," the sergeant agreed.

"She doesn't even remember who her birth mother was. All she remembers is our mom and dad now. But I'll talk to her."

"Does any one have any other questions?"

"How soon do you think it will be—this week or longer than that?" Jonathon asked.

"I'm going to try to arrange it next week. I think a week day would be better than a Saturday." Sergeant Larson stood up. "I hope I've answered all your questions. I know this is a surprise or possibly a shock to you two who thought the girl's mother had died and I'm sorry about that. Now, good evening and thank you for the delicious meal. It sure did taste good."

They watched the sergeant leave. No one said anything at first but Sabrina finally told them that it was her bed time and she was going to bed. Lisa hoped that she wouldn't have another nightmare about her mother.

"I wonder why Sabrina didn't want to talk anymore about her birth mother. Sometimes I don't understand her but she must have a reason," Lisa commented.

"Your daughter likes to think things over before she says or does anything. Give her time and she'll talk with you."

"Well, it's bed time. Let's go to bed. It's been a long evening." Jonathon was headed for the bedroom.

Lisa wanted to think about the evening for a while. To think that she tried so hard to get Sabrina to believe that her mother was dead, when all the time her mother was alive and Sabrina knew that. That was amazing. What was the woman like?

She hoped that Emma would like them and be pleased at how well her two children looked. What had the police told Emma about us? What did Emma expect from us?

One thing that Lisa was thankful for and that was that Emma didn't want to take the children away from their home. The woman had to love her children to be able to give them what was in their best interest.

The sergeant had suggested that they just use first names when they met Emma Brothers. He told her that Emma didn't want to know their last name or where they lived or anything. If Southerland ever did find her, somehow she believed he and his gang would want to do away with the children too. She'd rather live without them than put them in jeopardy. She was a good mother.

Lisa headed for the bedroom. She wondered if she'd sleep after hearing everything that the sergeant told them. As she lay in the bed trying to sleep she began to pray for Emma Brothers. The woman missed a great part of the girl's lives. She hoped that Emma was happy where she was.

Chapter Thirty

Meeting the Birth Mother

The following week, Sergeant Larson called and asked if the family would be ready for a trip the next day. Yes, they would Lisa answered.

"Sergeant, I take it this is a one day trip, right?" Lisa asked.

"That's right."

Lisa wanted the girls to look nice so she told them to dress in their prettiest clothes and she would fix their hair special. "Girls, I want you to be on your best behavior for this meeting. You're going to meet a special person and there is to be positively no arguing in front of this friend." Everyone agreed not to mention who they were meeting in front of Sissy.

"We won't argue," Sabrina promised. "We don't have to get fancy for this lady, mom. She's not a fancy person. You act like you're nervous. You shouldn't be. You'll like her, I'm sure."

"I just want you to look nice for her." Lisa noticed that when Sissy wasn't around Sabrina always referred to her mother as the birth mother. That was interesting. Perhaps she didn't want to hurt our feelings or she wanted us to know that she considered us as her real parents now.

When Jonathon arrived home, Lisa gave him the news. He called Joseph and asked if he and his son could watch the garage the next day that he had a trip he had to take. It sure was good to have some dependable employees and be able to leave the garage in their hands. Joseph was always willing to take on the responsibility of running the garage. Jonathon still believed he and his son worked late so they wouldn't have too many cars left when he returned to work after an absence.

A van came to the Livingston home the next morning. The family was all ready to take the trip to meet the children's birth mother. It was surprising that Sabrina said very little on the trip. Lisa would have thought that the girl would be a little excited but she wasn't. She could tell that her daughter was doing some deep thinking. Lisa would like to ask her what was bothering her but for some reason didn't think she should. It could be any number of things that might have happened in the past. Her daughter had too great of a memory for her own good.

It was a pleasant drive. Sergeant Larson was always entertaining. He kept the girls laughing even though with Sabrina it was a sober laugh. After pointing out the different sights along the way, he would ask if anyone wanted to stop.

"No," Sabrina answered. She wanted to get this over with. It had been over five years almost six since she had seen her mother. The girl had learned in Sunday school that you had to forgive someone if you were to be forgiven. Sabrina had asked Jesus to forgive her and she believed that He died on the cross for her sins. She knew that she was to forgive someone who did something against her and that would include her mother.

Remembering what her mother put the two girls through with her father and then running away from the safe house and not having food to eat were not pleasant memories. Could she forgive her mother? She had no choice if she wanted Jesus to forgive her. She would try hard to greet her mother and try to love her. This was one time she was glad that Sissy was too young to remember her mother or the terrible things they went through the first few years of their lives.

What she resented most was that her mother didn't do anything when her father hit them in the head or slapped them around when they did nothing to deserve it. Why didn't she stick up for them? Every time that happened, the mother just left and went into her room. Everything else was forgivable but this was something hard to forgive. Her mother should have stopped her father from hurting them.

By the time they reached the home where her mother lived, Sabrina had figured things out. She had prayed a silent prayer and she'd settled things in her mind.

The group entered the home. It was a place that held several different people, some of them had families but most of them were single.

The officer asked for Emma Brothers' apartment. The receptionist led them down the hall and knocked on the door. When Emma opened the door, she told her that her company had arrived. Emma invited the family to come in.

She hugged Sissy first and didn't want to release her. "You are such a pretty little girl. You've grown up so much. I see that you've been living with a nice mom and dad and I'm pleased about that. God has been good to you, Sissy." She hugged the girl one more time. Then Sissy played with her brother and didn't pay much attention to the conversation going on.

Emma put her arms out for Sabrina to get a hug. She wasn't sure the girl would hug her. She remembered the terrible quarrel they had because of what her father did to the two girls. Would her daughter forgive her?

Slowly, Sabrina walked over and gave her mother a quick hug. She knew it was expected of her. "Hello. I'm glad you have a nice place to live and people are taking care of you," Sabrina told her with little enthusiasm.

"They're very good to me, Sabrina. I want you to know that I've found Jesus Christ as my Savior. He has forgiven me of my sins and I have worked on forgiving your father for what he did to us. I'm so sorry the way he treated you and I didn't have the gumption to stop him. He would have only beat me and then come back and slapped you around some more. He started out a good man but he turned bad a few months after I married him. Can you forgive me, Sabrina?"

The girl looked at her mother. She said nothing for a while and then she remarked, "I'm trying."

"That's good enough. God will help you. You've grown into a beautiful young lady. You'll be eleven shortly and I want to give you a birthday present and one to Sissy as well." Emma took out two gifts and gave to the girls. Sissy's present was several Christian books for children about her age.

"Thank you for this present. I love to read," Sissy remarked.

Sabrina opened hers. It was the family picture album but missing was any picture of her father. She looked through it and saw when she was a baby and when Sissy was a baby. The girl was thrilled with the album.

"I thought you should have that. You need to have pictures of your first five years. Now would the whole family pose for me and let me take your picture now?" she asked.

Jonathon lined the girls up and then stepped into the picture. Emma snapped several shots.

"Now why don't you stand with the girls and let me take your picture?" Jonathon suggested.

Sissy held Emma's hand but Sabrina just stood beside her. Sissy grinned but Sabrina had a forced grin. She didn't particularly want to have her picture taken but she knew it was part of the process of forgiving so she went along with it.

"Now, I know you two have a good mother and father. I wonder if you could call me Aunt Emma. You don't have to Sabrina, but you need to call me something. Do you think you could call me Aunt Emma?"

Sissy replied without hesitation, "Yes, Aunt Emma, you're a nice person."

"Aunt Emma, thank you for the album. You couldn't give me anything that I would like more. I know that mom and dad will want to see the pictures and have me tell them what I know. Thank you again."

Emma was pleased that the girl appreciated the album. She was pretty sure she would but she also knew that Sabrina had carried a grudge against her so she didn't know how this visit was going to be. She prayed that the girl would learn to forgive.

It was past lunch time and Emma suggested they stay for lunch. She fixed some sandwiches, a drink and a desert. Lisa and Jonathon thought it was a good idea. They wondered what the two officers outside the door were going to do for lunch.

"Emma, do you have enough bread to make sandwiches for the two officers?" Jonathon asked.

"Oh, we planned this ahead of time. The owner of this place promised to feed the two gentlemen. They're well taken care of and they are getting to eat some hot food instead of sandwiches."

After the lunch was finished, the officers knocked on the door. "It's time to head back home. You have fifteen minutes to say your goodbyes," he told them.

"Thank you for letting me be with the girls. I hope that sometime they'll catch Ted Southerland and I'll be free to visit once in a while. I promise that I'll not bug you or be a nuisance. The girls have so much more than I ever gave them or could give them in the future and it isn't hard to see that they are well loved and that they love you. That was my prayer and God answered it."

"You're a brave woman," Lisa remarked. "You've done an unselfish thing for the girls and it couldn't have been easy. I'm not sure I could have done that. But thank you and we do love those two girls. They get high grades in their school work and they are very well behaved with the exception of a few sibling arguments but not all that many."

"The boy's name is Justin," Sabrina remarked.

"Let me give Justin a hug. He's been so good and hasn't said a thing. You sure are a cutie young man," she told Justin.

He just stared at her. He was at the age where he had to know someone before he accepted them. She kissed him on the cheek and he stared at her some more. He didn't like strange women kissing him.

Jonathon and Lisa laughed.

"Thanks again for coming. I know that you didn't have to agree to come and you had every right to turn me down. Thanks."

"You're very welcome. We hope to see you again one of these days. Take care, and may God bless you," Jonathon stated as they left the apartment.

No one said anything as they climb into the police unmarked vehicle.

After they were well on their way, Lisa remarked. "I don't think I could have given my children away no matter what," she whispered to Jonathon.

"Lisa, I think you would if you knew that someone was chasing you and perhaps the person would kill you and your children. She's a brave woman to do what she did," Jonathon remarked and Lisa agreed with him.

When they returned home it was late in the afternoon and everyone was tired. Lisa decided she would fix a simple dinner and they'd all go to bed early.

Jean knocked on the door. "Come in Jean," Lisa invited.

"Well, how was your trip? Everyone rested up?"

"I think everyone is very tired but it was a good trip. Just a lot of miles with a family but we enjoyed the day. I'm going to fix a little dinner and that's all I'm doing this evening."

"I figured you'd get in late, so I have dinner all ready for you. My table isn't big enough for all of you so do you want me to bring it out to your table?" Jean asked.

"That was so nice of you. I'll help you put it on the table. We're a bit tired," Lisa remarked again.

Jean had some pork steaks, rolls, mashed potatoes and gravy and a nice salad. After the blessing was said, everyone dug in. They weren't just tired, they were hungry and every thing Jean cooked smelled so good. Jean joined them as she often did. This time she was able to cook a whole meal for them and she was pleased.

"This is so good, Jean," Jonathon remarked.

Even Justin had a good appetite and was putting the food away. After dinner they felt a bit rested. After watching a little television they were all off to bed for a good night's sleep.

Chapter Thirty-One

The Boy with the Scars

Before they realized it, school was about to start up again. Sabrina would be in the sixth grade, Sissy in the third, and Justin would go to kindergarten. She would actually have a little spare time. Lisa thought she might even visit the garage. Of course Justin would only be going in the morning and would be home by noon.

Two weeks after school started, Lisa received a phone call from the judge.

"Lisa, my children's worker is away and there's a boy that needs to stay with someone until we find a home. He's eleven years old. Could you help me out? You can look over the prospective parents but I'm afraid there aren't too many who want to take in a child that old."

"Sure, bring him out. We'll take care of him until we find someone who does want him," Lisa answered.

"It will be this evening when he comes. Now I want you to know that he's been treated horrible by his parents and relatives along with the foster homes he was put in. He has bruises and cut marks all over him. He needs to feel he is loved by someone. I know you two will give him a lot of love while you're taking care of him."

"We'll treat him special and try to make him understand that we care. I'll be ready for him tonight."

Lisa was glad she had an extra bedroom. She was always going to separate the girls and give them separate rooms but they balked at that so she said no more. They were close sisters in spite of the difference in their ages.

Jonathon came home before the child arrived and Lisa told him all about him coming so he would be prepared. She told him how mistreated the boy had been. That was something Jonathon couldn't understand. Why did anyone want to be cruel to children?

"The judge said it would be after dinner and the boy would be fed dinner before he came," Lisa informed them so they sat down to an early dinner. After dinner they cleared away the dishes and went to watch the television. Lisa wasn't quite sure when the boy would show up. Why didn't she ask his name?

At eight o'clock an officer delivered the boy. He knocked on the door and Lisa invited him in. "This is Timothy Allan Smith."

"Hello, Timothy, welcome to our home," Lisa said and the boy smiled.

The officer left immediately and hoped the boy would be all right in that home. He sure hated seeing the marks all over the boy. Situations like this one was what made his job tougher than it should be. He loved children and the idea that some one would mistreat them didn't go over with him.

Jonathon walked over to him and Timothy backed away from him. His eyes widened and Jonathon could tell that the boy was frightened of him. "Son, I'd never hurt you. Please don't be afraid of me. I love children and I love boys. Now, let's go into the family room and get a little acquainted."

"You're not going to hit me?" he asked.

"I'd never hit you, Timothy. Look at our children. There are no marks on them. They're happy in our home and we want to make you happy."

Timothy looked at him almost disbelieving him.

"Pickup your suitcase and let me show you your room first," Jonathon suggested.

Timothy did but Jonathon could still see some fear in the boy but he did follow Jonathon into the bedroom.

"This is your bedroom. I'll help you hang up your clothes or put them in the dresser. Now do you need a shower before going to bed?"

"I had one down at the police station," he answered.

"What grade are you in?"

"Do I have to go to school?" Timothy asked.

"The law requires that you do," Jonathon said. "However, we can home school you if you wish."

Jonathon saw relief wash over the boy's face. "When I go to a public school, I have to undress for gym and everyone sees my back. It's embarrassing."

Jonathon put his arm around the boy. "I'm so sorry for the life you had to live but here you won't have to worry about getting slapped around or beaten. I don't do that to children, Timothy. I hope I can make you believe me." He hugged the boy.

Much to his surprise, Timothy hugged him back. "Now the family is going to watch a movie and then go to bed. Sometimes we have a little dessert while we watch television. Do you want to join us?"

"I'd love to," Timothy said enthusiastically. He might like this house. The man sure seems nice and he had a room all to himself. He never did before. He had to share it with two or three other boys who were older and mean to him. He wondered how long these people would keep him. The judge said they would find a place for him. So far he liked this home and wouldn't mind staying here.

He laughed through the movie with the other three children along with the parents. Jonathon always liked to have a family time when they could work it in. Sometimes they watch TV together and other times they did projects. They even did picture puzzles together.

Before everyone went to their room, Jonathon had a time of prayer. He prayed for each member of the family and then for Timothy. He prayed that he would be happy in his new home and would realize that Jesus loved him.

Jonathon went with Timothy to his new room. "Could I look at your sores, Timothy, and make sure they're not infected?"

"A policeman took me to the hospital and they fixed me up. Some of the sores were infected and they gave me some medicine to put on them. They said to leave the bandages on them until tomorrow."

"I see you have some patches on your arms. Who did this to you?"

"My dad did. He'd get drunk and beat me. I tried to run away but he always found me and forced me to come back to his house."

"Do you have a mother?"

"No, she died. He beat her too."

Jonathon did all he could to keep the tears out of his eyes. "Well, Timothy, you're going to live a different life now."

"But what about when they move me to another place. I've been to two different homes and both of the men smacked me around. And then the people would send me back to my father. I wish I could stay with you. You pray to God and you prayed for me. Thank you."

"I'll talk to my wife. As for me, I want to keep you. We have to go to the judge and get his okay."

"You mean you really want me to live with you?" the boy asked.

"I sure do."

"I want you to live with us too," Lisa stated. "I happened to be passing by the bedroom and heard you two talking. We want to protect you from any more bad treatment, Timothy. You've seen the worst in people. It's time you saw the good people and there are a lot of them in the world."

"Lisa, would you mind home schooling him. Because of his scars, he doesn't want to go to regular school where he'd have to undress for the physical education classes."

"I'd be pleased to home school you. Maybe we could even go to Jonathon's garage some time and study there. Did you know that he was a mechanic?"

"The judge told me."

Jonathon hugged him good night and then Lisa did. The boy looked up and smiled at both of them. He couldn't remember in his whole life someone treating him this special.

He only hoped that the judge would let him stay at this house. He sure liked the other children. Justin was a fun kid to play with. He was awful little and that made him all the more fun to be with. If these people kept him, Justin would be his little brother. It would be nice to have a brother.

Chapter Thirty-Two

One More Adoption

Judge Watson wasn't surprised to see Jonathon and Lisa along with Timothy come into his courtroom.

"I've been expecting you," the judge smiled. "How do you like the Livingston family, Timothy?"

"They are nice people, judge," he answered.

"Now what can I do for you two?"

"We want to adopt Timothy," Jonathon remarked. He knew that the judge wasn't the least bit surprised. That was why he had sent the boy to them. He knew we were tender hearted toward children and after hearing about all of the boy's wounds, we'd want to protect him.

"I can't say that I'm surprised, Jonathon. It just so happens I have the paper work all filled out and all I need is your signature."

Jonathon and Lisa grinned at the judge. They weren't too surprised at what the judge did before even asking them if they wanted to adopt the boy. That judge knew them a little too well. "Now judge, this makes four children. That's enough," Jonathon suggested.

"If you say so," smiled Judge Watson. He knew the next poor victim that came into his court that needed a loving home would probably be sent to them to stay overnight. "Timothy comes with free medical care. He has some bad bruises and cuts and it will take some time before they are healed."

Jonathon and Lisa signed the paper and then hugged the boy.

"Can I call you mom and dad," Timothy asked.

"That's what we are so of course you can call us that," Jonathon answered.

They left the court house and returned home. The other children were all in school. Lisa knew she had to apply for home schooling and get the required material to teach the boy. He said he was in the sixth grade. She'd do that today.

"Timothy, since you don't have your books yet to study, how about coming with me to the garage today. You can see what I do. You never know, you just may make a good mechanic someday," Jonathon remarked.

"I'd like that. That would be fun."

The two left for the garage and Lisa left to check on the home schooling for sixth graders. Since she did some home schooling herself, she knew a little what to do although she had a real teacher and followed what the school was teaching.

Timothy watched what Jonathon was doing. He watched Joseph and Jacob. When Jacob went to vacuum a car Timothy asked if he could vacuum the car. Jacob looked at Jonathon and he nodded his head.

When he finished Jonathon inspected the car. "You did a good job. Would you like to wash the outside?"

Timothy's eyes widened. "Yes, I know how to do that."

Jonathon noticed that the boy was doing a good job. "Hey you two I think we just might have discovered another mechanic to work here in the garage. Look how well he did this car."

Jacob and Joseph both praised the boy. "You've done a fine job," Joseph remarked and patted the boy on the back.

Timothy winced.

"Joseph, he has some bad sores on his back that need to be healed up. When they are healed we'll all give him a pat on the back.

"I'm sorry, Timothy, I didn't know."

Jonathon showed him how to change the oil in a car and watched him as he carefully accomplished the job. Timothy had a smile a mile wide. He loves all of this, thought Jonathon.

"Timothy, have you ever been around cars much?"

"No, but that's what I wanted to do. I want to be a mechanic as I love cars," he stated enthusiastically.

Timothy proved to be an apt student and completed his studies every night. Lisa was pleased that she had no trouble with him. He wanted to work in the garage with Jonathon in the day time and do his homework in the evening. They told him as long as he finished all his school work on time, he could do that.

The boy entered into playing with the other three children. He often taught them new games. After the month, he was just another member to the family and felt at home with the Livingstons. He also enjoyed his new grandmother who was always doing something special for him.

A year later the door bell rang and Jonathon answered it. When he asked the man to step in, he heard Timothy yell. "Don't come in here. Go away. I don't ever want to see you," the boy yelled.

"I don't care what you want you're coming home with me now. You're my son and you had no business running away and being put in another foster home. Now get your things and come with me now."

Jonathon stepped closer to the man. He was small in statue while Jonathon was a good sized man. He looked down on him and said very softly, "That's my son as I've adopted him. He's lived here for a year. Now you'll leave and never come back. If you don't, I'll call the police."

The man paled. He knew the police were looking for him but he needed his son. He didn't want to do all the work that he had to do without any help. "This isn't over," the man said and left.

Timothy ran to Jonathon and hugged him. "I was so scared," he exclaimed. "I didn't want to go back to his house and I was afraid he'd make me."

"You're my son, Timothy. No one can take you away from me. I don't believe he'll come back. Lisa has called the police and told them the car license plate number. I imagine you know he's been in prison and I'm not sure how he got out. I think he'll be picked up by the police very soon. Part of the plea bargain he made was to give up all rights to you so you could be adopted."

Timothy was thankful that his dad probably would never come after him again.

"Jonathon, how is Timothy doing as a mechanic after a year working down there? He's only twelve," Lisa asked.

"Lisa, he can do anything that is needed to be done on a vehicle. He's a whiz and I understand he's getting good grades on his school homework. We got us a good mechanic and a scholar and a great son."

When Justin was ten, he decided he didn't want to be a mechanic. It was fun to visit the garage but he didn't care about the work. He wanted to be a school teacher, he informed his dad. That was all right with Jonathon.

The new garage had been built a few years ago and the four mechanics were taking care of the vehicles that came to the garage for repair. Jonathon knew that he could easily get away. He almost felt not needed at the garage anymore.

Sabrina was in college and Sissy was in high school now. Justin was a few years behind them. Timothy home schooled the whole time. He wanted to be a mechanic and he didn't want that to be interrupted by having to attend school every day. He promised to get some college at night school and the parents agreed.

They didn't intend to have four children, Lisa thought, but all four of them were the best children that anyone could ask for. She hoped that the judge never called again for them to take a child over night. One night and they didn't want to give the children up. Perhaps they should change their phone number and not let the judge know. She smiled. She had an idea there'd be one or two more children that would need a home and they'd probably give them one. It appeared that most people wanted babies to adopt but when the child was older, they weren't interested.

Jonathon and Lisa loved their family. They were growing up a little too fast and they realized that one day, they would have an empty nest. About that time, the judge would probably call.